Gold DIGGER

Finding the gold is easy.
Keeping it will be
the challenge.

Andrene Low

All names, characters, places, and incidents in this publication are fictitious or are used fictitiously. Any resemblance to real persons, living or dead, events or locales is entirely coincidental.

That Seventies Series – Comprising Heels and a Tiara, Friday Night Fever, Brush With Fame, Strapped for Cash, Out of Bounds, Maid in Chelsea and Gold Digger.

© 2017-2020 by Andrene Low

All rights reserved under International and Pan-American Copyright Conventions. By payment of the required fees, you have been granted the non-exclusive, non-transferable right to access and read the text of this e-book on-screen. No part of this text may be reproduced, transmitted, downloaded, decompiled, reverse engineered, or stored in or introduced into any information storage and retrieval system, in any form or by any means, whether electronic or mechanical, now known or hereinafter invented, without the express written permission of the author.

ISBN: 978-0-9951388-8-9

1

Stef twirls the paddle to check its weight, unable to stop a snigger. If it wasn't for all the studs peppering one side, she could be getting ready for a game of ping pong.

Instead, she's readying herself for a game of *paddle pops*. The spanking paddle atop her haphazardly folded clothes, she closes the lid on her suitcase. Once she's checked it's properly locked, she rolls it out onto the landing.

The old-school metal skates taped to the bottom with a bucket-load of electrical tape are the work of her dad. He'd learned a thing or two in his years as a London cabbie, and how to avoid lugging bags was top of the list. Sure, it looks a sight, but it works.

Back in her room, Stef lifts the blankets on her bed and, sliding her hand in underneath the bottom sheet, retrieves a dog-eared manila folder. It's the only one she kept after she, Brenda, and Julian lifted a whole pile from Wallace Smythe-Brown's London town house. Its current condition isn't how they'd found it but courtesy of the number of times she's flicked through its contents.

She doesn't need to read through everything again, pretty much knowing it all off by heart. However, this doesn't stop her from a quick skim. She probably knows the contents better than Wallace *Shit-Brown* and that pug-ugly nephew of his, Rupert. These two being the reprobates who'd compiled all the dossiers.

Just like the others, the papers she's flicking through were used to blackmail a member of the British aristocracy out of his hard-earned coin. But with her about to visit Cecil Percy-Ryder, the subject of this very dossier, she can't risk taking it with her. She's going to have to rely on her memory this time.

Her gaze keeps going back to the one term that pops up over and over. It sounds so familiar, but she can't for the life of her think why. "Arthur's Folly? Arthur's Folly?" No matter how many times she says it aloud, or in her head, she still can't get the connection. The memory of hearing these words spoken when she was a child has stuck, just not the setting or who it was who said them. She shakes her head, hoping to rattle some brain cells free, but it does no good. On shoving the file back in its hiding spot she's none the wiser.

A quick shufty at her new, upmarket watch—a recent gift from Cecil—and Stef realises she needs to get a wriggle-on. She'll cop grief from her dad if she's not downstairs and ready for him to take her to the train station. After struggling down the stairs with her suitcase, she marvels at how quiet the house is. The unearthly hush down to nearly all the inhabitants either being out of town or even out of the country. The only exceptions are Flo and Bert, the live-in help, and Eadie, her landlady and mentor.

Her case next to the front door, Stef taps gently on the sitting-room door. Last thing she needs is to scare the old girl and have to resort to her recently acquired CPR skills. "You awake, Eadie?" An unladylike snort from inside the room is all she needs to feel comfortable pushing the door open and walking in. "Right, I'm off to Cecil's pile in the country."

"You've got everything?"

Stef nods, part of her still in disbelief that the genteel looking octogenarian sitting in front of her is the one who's been responsible for her dominatrix training. Although even she realises, she's still got a lot to learn. Never in a million years could she have seen this future for herself when she was approached by that crazy Aussie bird, Brenda, a mere couple of months back.

Still, it beats living at home in a moth-eaten part of East London where all the household appliances are hot. Not temperature wise, rather due to a dad who keeps finding things before they've even been 'lost'. It's also a lot better than working as a barmaid; with less time on her feet, and tips a zillion times greater.

Perhaps the biggest surprise, or is that another plus, is that she doesn't have to shag the old guys, just paddle their flabby arses. Her telling them they've been a very bad boy in her sternest voice possible doesn't go astray, either. The hardest part is not laughing when they respond like a schoolboy who's been caught doing something naughty.

And being paid in cash or trinkets also has

her managing to save, for the first time in her life.

After clocking the half-empty decanter on the small table next to Eadie's chair, Stef asks, "You all good for sherry?"

"If you could just top up my glass that would be wonderful. Flo will be back from the shops soon and she can take care of things after that."

Even with Brenda's school for girls no longer in operation Eadie's domestics, Flo and Bert, have continued to live on the premises. It's something all the girls are happy about. Knowing that Eadie, who they all love and who's got crippling arthritis, has round-the-clock support gives them peace of mind.

Stef does as she's asked, before bending down and kissing the old lady's cheek, surprising both of them. "You take care of ya-self while I'm away."

Rather than respond in words, Eadie waves toward the door, shooing Stef out of the room to a background of jaunty beeping from her dad out front.

. . .

Stef pauses on the front step, waiting for it to dawn on her dad that she's not lugging her suitcase down the path to his car. This takes longer than it should, perhaps in part due to his general avoidance of hard work.

"Blimmin' 'eck, love, whatcha got in here, a body?"

"That's why I needed a ride. Didn't want to hav'ta deal with it on the tube."

She's close enough to hear him muttering about 'a bloody hearse' when he manhandles it through the back door and onto the seat. His avoiding putting her bag in the boot means one of two things. He doesn't fancy lifting it up and into the boot or the boots chocker with stuff that's hot enough to blister the paintwork.

They're nearly at the station before Stef broaches the subject she's been mulling over and the whole reason she wanted a ride with her dad. "Da?"

"Yes, love."

"Do the words *Arthur's Folly* mean anything to ya?"

His reaction is such that she immediately regrets asking him while he's driving. They're lucky there's no-one next to them when he swerves wildly.

"Where the bleedin' 'ell?" He chokes off the rest of his comment, takes a couple of deep breaths and starts up again. "Why'd ya ask love?" His tone is suspiciously neutral.

This is part of what Stef has been contemplating over. Her pulling the wool over her old man's eyes is never easy, and with him on high alert like he is now, it'll be even harder.

"Relax, would ya! I had a dream about it. Last night."

If there's one thing Brenda's taught her, it's that there's nothing like going on the attack to throw someone off the scent and so she goes in for the kill. "Da, you carryin' on like this has me thinking I musta heard it from you."

Damn, his eye's twitching. Wait for it. Wait for it.

"Not me, love. You musta imagined it."

Now she knows she's onto something. While Brenda has taught her how to run a good offence, it's her mum who's shown her how to run defence. That woman can get information out of her dad even when he doesn't want to give up.

. . .

Her suitcase safely stowed in the baggage car, and herself ensconced in a first-class compartment, Stef sinks back into her seat. Her mind full of whirling images of what her dad told her in the car. It's unbelievable and a sure thing that Wallace and Rupert Smythe-Brown don't know about it, or they'd have blackmailed her elderly friend into coughing up for sure.

Fortunately, with those two reprobates in the pokey, it leaves the way clear for her to snoop around at Cecil's without risk of being sprung. She'd be nervous if they'd simply done a 'Lord Lucan', with the number of purported sightings of that supposedly dead peer indicating there's no way he's topped himself; just faked it.

The trip is uneventful. The train leaves ten minutes late proving that, even with a first-class ticket, British Rail lives up to its reputation. Perhaps it's because it's two in the afternoon on a Tuesday, but Stef has the compartment to herself for the entire trip. Perfect as far as she's concerned, saving her from having to make small talk with people she's got nothing in common with. It's not as if she can come clean on what she'll do while she's in the country. Well, not without having her fellow passengers jumping off the train next time it so much as slows down.

On disembarking at the small station Cecil told her is close to Ryder Hall, Stef drags her bag from where it's been dumped. She tugs it along the platform, doing her best to ignore the squeaky wheels, and into a small, but surprisingly tidy, waiting room.

And there she waits.

And waits.

Surely Cecil doesn't expect her to spring for a taxi, if such a service is even available out here? Dammit, she doesn't even have a phone number for the house. If he's not here soon, she'll teach him a lesson by catching the first train back to town.

She's worn quite the groove in the wide wooden floor boards when a man explodes into the waiting room, looking wildly around. Thanks to the size of the room, and her being the only one in it, his gaze locks onto her immediately.

"Stefanie!?"

She tilts her head back in order to examine his face. It's an unfamiliar action for her when she's wearing stilettoes. Unable to respond verbally, her words jammed firmly in her throat, she gives him a curt nod. It's enough to have him grabbing the handle of her large suitcase and lifting it as though it doesn't weigh a ton. And yet another reason to have her heart beating double-time.

Steff trails him out of the waiting room, all while struggling to get herself under control. It's been a long time since a man's affected her this way, and especially not after he's only barked one word at her. *Could it be because I've only been interacting with submissive older gents for the past couple of months? Yes. That must be it.*

Nothing at all to do with the guy being built like a brick shit house and too rough around the edges to appear on the cover of a romance novel. Watching the muscles in his back ripple when he hefts her suitcase into a beaten-up Land Rover, Stef's unable to stop a sharp intake of breath. It's something that has him turning and examining her in a manner that leaves her feeling uncomfortable.

Might he know why I'm here? For the first time since she started down her new career path, her profession doesn't sit comfortably, a rampant flush starting between her boobs and travelling north. The brow he arches in question isn't easy to spot, hidden as it is under an unruly mop of dark hair.

"Must be coming down with something."

He doesn't appear to be buying it. Instead he passes deliberately close by her on his way to the passenger's door. He then gestures with his free hand for her to get in, all with a smug grin plastered on that chiselled face of his. *Damn.*

On taking in the state of the front seat, Stef stalls. There's no way she's getting in there and sitting on all that crud in her brand-new Burberry trench coat. A heartfelt sigh from behind her, she steps to the side. She's relieved when he reaches over the back of the seats and grabs a towel. After ridding the seat of dirt and grime, he gives the towel a vigorous shake before folding it carefully and placing it on the seat for her to sit on.

Despite all this, she knows that she won't be comfortable sitting this close to him during the drive. Not when she's on her way to cater to the sexual needs of an old bloke, using a paddle and handcuffs. Unfortunately, the Land Rover doesn't have any back seats, and she sure as heck isn't riding in the tray with her suitcase.

And being strapped across the bonnet is definitely not happening, unless it's Cecil and she's in charge of the rope.

The cab feels even smaller when he climbs in the driver's side and settles himself behind the wheel. It's odd being cast in the subservient role after playing the 'Dom' for the preceding two months. She can't work out whether she likes it or not, and isn't keen on examining it too closely.

The drive is completed in silence, neither of them saying a word until the Land Rover swings through the gates at Ryder Hall. Then there's not a hope she can stay quiet. "Bleedin' 'ell!" The drive goes on forever, protected from the elements by a colonnade of ancient oak trees. But it's not this that's been responsible for Stef's oath, it's that through the trees she's got a gander of the main house and it's humongous. Even bigger than the place she'd visited with Brenda, Julian, and the other girls for the country house party.

It's not a friendly house, with nothing wedding cake about it. It's shrouded in 'glum', the stone dark with age and featuring enough pointy bits to give off a dangerous vibe simply sitting there. If it's this dismal from the outside, gawd only knows what it'll be like inside.

She quietly soaks everything in, and boy is there a lot of it. She was aware Cecil was rich, but this is not what she's been expecting. As foreboding as it is, she can understand why he chooses to spend most of his time in the city. Other than at the height of summer, or over Christmas when family are in residence, he steers clear of the place.

Obviously, he's making an exception for her visit because it is neither the height of summer nor Christmas time. She can't complain, with fewer people she can check out what her dad told her about in the car. Jeez, if he knew what information he'd innocently handed her, he'd blow a gasket.

They're driving across the broad expanse of gravel that fronts the house when she spots a Roman ruin off to the right. There's no doubt the hillock it sits atop is manmade. "What's that?" She's 95% sure she knows, although she's unable to stop herself from holding her breath until it's confirmed.

Her driver turns in the direction she's pointing. "That?" He harrumphs in disgust before continuing, "That's Arthur's Folly."

2

It's no surprise the B&D paraphernalia Eadie has lent her is as heavy as it is. There's nothing cheap about any of it, with everything made out of thick leather and sporting enough buckles to keep the naughtiest of boys under control.

From what Cecil had said, he's got everything she needs, but Eadie had insisted she pack things she's comfortable with. Her as new to the scene as she is, it's her preference too. Thank goodness the driver had carried it up to her room, or she'd be a heaving, sweaty mess right now. She still doesn't know what his name is and she's damned if she'll ask.

Stef lays her equipment out on the large four-poster, a smile flickering across her face. By the time she's finished with Cecil, he'll be gagging to tell her all about Arthur's Folly. She knows she didn't get the complete picture from her dad because, even while he'd been spilling his guts, that damned eye of his had never fully quietened down. Her mum said if it was flickering, he was holding back. No, it will be up to her to put the pieces together. If the treasure is what her dad makes it out to be, she's gonna need a blasted wheelbarrow to move it all.

She's had a good nosy around her room, unpacked her suitcase, slid it under the bed and is lying back taking in the room when there's a discrete knock at her bedroom door. About time the old codger turned up. She's already been here nearly half-an-hour.

Once again standing, Stef gives herself a mental shake, and dons her dominatrix persona. It's show-time. Stalking across the bedroom in ground-eating strides, she wrenches the door open wide and yells "Where the hell have you been?!"

The driver doesn't respond other than opening and closing his mouth a few times.

"Oh shit, sorry. I thought you were Cecil." This does nothing to explain away her oddball behaviour, at least not if the puzzlement on his face is any indicator.

"Drinks are being served in the conservatory, if you'd like to make your way downstairs."

With his tone brusque and his departure immediate, Stef's none the wiser as to where the conservatory is, or even if he's accepted her apology. She couldn't have accompanied him anyway. She's wearing little more than a leather corset and lacy knickers underneath the Burberry coat that's, thankfully, still buttoned up.

Unaware if there'll be anyone else at the drinks, Stef flies over to the freestanding wardrobe and yanks the door open. She then flicks through the clothes she's just put in there. Thank goodness Eadie had told her to pack a few dresses, with it being a demure dark plum number she grabs now.

The trench coat tossed over the end of the bed, she doesn't bother removing the leather corset before throwing the dress on. She's still buttoning it up on her way out the door. She manages to retrace her steps to the main foyer but, as to where she's meant to go from here, she's at a loss. Well, not completely. She's watched as many BBC period dramas as the next girl and knows the conservatory will be at the back of the house. Question is how to reach the back of the house without going out the front door around the side of the building and finding it that way.

She's opened the fifth door leading off the main hall before she strikes gold, with the room she's entered opening out onto the conservatory. The murmur of male voices as she crosses the lushly carpeted room has her glad she's wearing the dress over her B&D get-up.

Stef pauses on the threshold to the conservatory. This gives her eyes time to adjust to the increase in light. Only then does she walk down the wide concrete steps and between towering palms in the direction of the other guests. She recognises Cecil's voice but is unsure who it is he's talking to, with their conversation having stopped abruptly when her heels had first clattered against the tiled floor. Long enough though for her to hear Cecil say, "Arthur wouldn't like that". There's that blasted name again.

On turning a corner on the meandering path she's been following, Stef feels like she stumbled into a scene from a Somerset Maugham play. Cecil sits at his ease in a large fan-backed cane chair, a cigar in one hand.

What looks like a glass of whisky is gripped in the other.

"Hello dear, I was thinking about sending young Liam in search of you."

Next to Cecil's chair, Stef bends down and gives him a daughterly kiss on the forehead. It's only when she straightens that she gets to see who the occupant of the other Peacock chair is. She's not often surprised, but seeing the driver sitting at his ease and armed with a cigar and a glass of whisky does it. Isn't that taking fraternising with the staff a step too far?

Cecil waves his cigar in the younger man's direction. "I believe you've already made the acquaintance of Liam, my sister's boy."

"Not officially," says Stef, unable to stop herself from sounding a little sniffy. *Why the hell hadn't he said who he was when he picked me up at the station? Hmmmph, letting me think he was the hired help.* A brief glance in his direction and she knows full well the bastard's done it on purpose.

"Help yourself to a small libation, dear." Cecil once again uses his cigar as a pointer. "We're not hung up on protocol down here in the country."

Small libation? Stef could murder a pint of

Watney's bleedin' red barrel but a glass of whisky will have to do, given this is all that's on offer. She doesn't hold back, filling her glass indecently close to the top. She thinks twice about nabbing a cigar from the case but decides no before taking the only unoccupied cane chair.

Cecil proceeds to lead their conversation, covering off the weather, her train journey down, and gossip about people they both know. Liam doesn't utter a word, instead keeping his gaze on Stef whilst drinking his whisky and drawing on his cigar, to the point she's squirming. She's used to men checking her out, but this is more closely aligned to a scientific examination than ogling and she doesn't like it.

"Well Liam, we won't keep you any longer. I'm sure you've got better things to do than sit here chewing the fat with us."

There's nothing veiled about Cecil's dismissal of his nephew, with it being blatant enough that the most socially inept would catch on.

"No, I'm fine. Been rushing all day." The younger man reinforces his intention to stay put by topping up his drink and even waving the decanter around in invitation.

"Come my dear," says Cecil. "Let me show you around the place."

Watching the old bloke dragging himself to his feet is painful, but Stef isn't about to offer any help and blow her dominant role. She does however worry if the cane chair is up to the challenge of him leaning fully on it. It's creaking alarmingly; almost as much as the old codger himself.

Only when he's safely on his pins and holding his arm out to her, does she stand, taking the opportunity to glance in Liam's direction. He's still staring at her.

What is his problem?

Cecil doesn't say another word until they're safely out in the front hall. "I do apologise for our unwanted company. Pops up like the harbinger of doom every time I want to have a little fun."

Stef's guarded in her response, only giving a small shrug. Not for a second does she think Liam won't follow them. Nope, until she knows what the full story is with that one, she's staying mum.

Cecil keeps up a running commentary on every bit of masonry on show, plus a few bits that aren't. All while walking determinedly across the hall toward a set of double doors on the far side. Rather than walking through them, he stops bang in front of the wall to the right. After some sleight of hand she hears a soft click, after which he pushes on a panel and stands back to allow it to swing out. He puts his finger to his lips and gestures for her to walk through the gap.

She wastes no time stepping into the relative dark, with Cecil close on her heels. The panel has only just clicked back into place when they hear a door opening out in the hallway and hurried steps. That it's Liam is confirmed when they hear him cursing, followed by a lot of opening and closing of doors. This is soon followed by the front door slamming hard enough to rattle the glass in the side panels.

Stef's about to speak, when Cecil places his finger over her lips, and she nods to let him know she's understood. Sure enough, another minute or two pass and then they hear the front door open and close again, this time more sedately.

"Right, let's get this show on the road," says Cecil, keeping his voice low as though still unsure if the coast is actually clear. The space is then illuminated when he clicks on a torch, flashing it around wildly and nearly clobbering her with it in the process.

Worried he's getting over-excited, Stef growls deep in the back of her throat before gritting out "Behave yourself!" It's enough to have him settling down, squeezing past her and leading the way down some stairs just beyond where they've been standing. The further they descend, the colder it gets and Stef wishes she'd worn her trench coat to drinks and stuff what Liam thought about it.

On stepping down into a dank cellar, Stef's relieved when Cecil flicks on some lights and hangs the torch on a nail sticking dangerously out of a nearby post. The extra light does nothing to help make the space cosy. Cecil must notice her shivering, because the next thing she knows a musty cape is draped around her shoulders. Watching him don a similar cape, she ties the ribbons at the neck of her own to hold it in place. When he pulls his hood up, Stef follows suit because, while it reeks of mould and days of old, the cape is fur lined and already warming her up.

What follows is a forced march, along a brick-lined passage that goes on for ever and is cold enough that her breath is visible in the dim light. Her stilettos no doubt make it feel further than it is, and she's careful where she puts her feet. And it's a challenge avoiding all the gaps between the flagstones. Of as much concern as ruining her new shoes, is Cecil's breathing. It's getting worse by the yard and Stef's giving thought to chucking the old chap over a shoulder and legging it, when she spots steps ahead.

There are a lot more steps at this end of the passage than there had been at the other. For once she avoids her dominant role. "Mind if we take a small breather before we tackle that lot?"

That Cecil doesn't answer other than to nod his agreement doesn't come as a surprise. If Stef was wheezing that hard, she wouldn't be able to talk either.

They have to stop twice more before they make it to the top of the steps and along a short corridor. There, Cecil pushes on a door, swinging it wide and standing to the side to allow her to enter first.

"Welcome, my dear. Welcome to Arthur's Folly."

3

Nope, it's not what Stef has been expecting at all. Rather than a high-end summer house, as the outside design would suggest, the inside is set up like a shrine. A shrine to having your arse paddled 'til pink.

To having weights and pulleys attached to bits and bobs that shouldn't have weights and pulleys attached to them. To featuring more stuff designed to inflict pain than is commonly seen outside the Tower of London.

She is way out of her league with this lot.

No wonder Eadie had suggested she bring her own gear. Liam would have a fit if he knew about this place. *Shit.*

"Liam doesn't know about this place, does he?"

Cecil, who's reclining on a fainting couch as if he's about to use it for its intended purpose, rouses himself enough to answer. "Good god, no. Not when the place got its name, courtesy of his father's actions. Mind if I have a little shuteye?"

He doesn't wait for her to answer before closing his eyes and snuggling into the depths of the fur-lined cloak that all but smothers his small frame.

Now what?

Stef wanders aimlessly around the room to a background of Cecil's gentle snoring, then there's nothing aimless about her actions. Despite searching Ryder Hall extensively, none of her dad's ah *colleagues* had ever been able to find their way into the Folly and so it's virgin territory in some respects. If it moves, she moves it. If it lifts, she lifts it to the best of her abilities, which are many after years of manhandling casks of beer in the basement of various pubs in London. Things that can slide are slid.

Nothing. Not even a bloody dust mote meaning someone on the staff knows about the place or Cecil likes to play maid while being whipped.

And if that's the case, I should get him around to clean my room at Eadie's place. Hell, Eadie would probably be happy if he cleaned the whole place from top to bottom.

Only two things are certain. She needs to get a fire going if they're to avoid freezing to death and, when she's done that, she's ditching the heels. No point being dominant when your submissive is out for the count and likely to remain that way for some time.

Half an hour later and there's a fire going that's got the combustive powers of something able to roast a whole pig. Even then, it doesn't stand a chance against the cold in this mausoleum of pain. Cecil peacefully asleep, Stef drags the chaise, with him atop, nearer to the fire without waking him.

For herself she shoves a small rack closer to the fire so she can sit on the end of it. There being sod all firewood left in the basket on the hearth, she'll use it for fuel if push comes to shove.

Even though she's sitting her feet still hurt. Sure, putting her shoes back on when Cecil rouses himself will hurt like the dickens, but better to have relief now while he's out for the count. After taking them off, she puts them carefully to one side and slides her feet out toward the flames, wiggling her toes to get some blood flowing. It's only when she's sliding her feet backward and forward to massage her heels that she notices something.

She bends forward, touching first one tile and then the other.

That's weird. They appear the same. *Shouldn't they all feel the same?*

Not until she's down on her hands and knees is she able to see the difference. While one is terracotta, the other is only painted to mimic terracotta. Stef swings around and unhooks one of the clamps from side of the rack. She then gets stuck into the grout, all while keeping as quiet as she can. This way she'll both avoid waking Cecil and hear if there's a hitch in his breathing to show he's about to wake up of his own accord.

It takes close to a half an hour to free the tile, but it's the highest hourly rate she's ever achieved. While the top of the tile gives the impression of terracotta, the weight and sheen of gold on the bottom tell her it's anything but. It's a few years' pay, that's what it is.

Now what? Stef turns the tile over and over in her hand, her mind whirling just as much. It's heavy, but not that heavy. And if there's one, there could be more. The way her dad had told it, the robbers had gotten away with a truckload. Not literally, just in matters of the overall value.

Cecil snorting and fidgeting is enough to let her know she doesn't have the luxury of time. Without pause, she lays the tile on the floor, ditches the cape, and unbuttons the front of her dress. Once free of it, she slides the tile down the front of her leather corset resulting in an intake of breath sharp enough to have her coughing.

She's only just managed to get the cape back in place when Cecil opens his eyes. There's only one way she'll avoid killing the old geezer today, and that's by playing her dominant role to the hilt.

Stef leaps to her feet, puts her hands on her hips and opens the cape enough that he can clock her red and black corset. "How dare you lay there like an odious slug while I wait!?"

"Sorry mistress."

"Do you know what I do to odious little slugs who keep me waiting?" Stef doesn't care what he answers; she'll do what she wants, anyway. And that's ignoring any of the B&D gear scattered around the Folly like toys abandoned after an ice cream truck passes the house.

"Whip me?" Cecil's voice if full of hope, as are his eyes.

Boy, are you in for a major letdown.

If Stef was to get physical now, the tile of gold would likely drop out the bottom of her corset, breaking a toe. Only by pushing her tummy out is she able to keep it nice and snug under her boobs.

"No, you little weasel. I've been waiting on you for over an hour. You'll get nothing tonight."

His disappointment is palpable and Stef pauses and sighs dramatically. It's enough that the gold tile slips just a smidgeon letting her know she's got no choice if she wants to keep her mitts on it. Who knows when, if ever, she'll gain access to Arthur's Folly again? "How dare you stare at me that way! For that, you can walk all the way back to the cellar in *my* shoes. Let's see how you like that."

. . .

Stef walks down the stairs ahead of Cecil, her feet snug and comfortable in Cecil's fashionable brogues. They're loose, although not so much she's unable to walk in them. Shame the same can't be said for Cecil, who's following behind her. He'd been unsteady and uncomfortable in her heels in the Folly, having her decide to lead the way. If he took a header from top step to bottom, there'd be no way he'd survive.

They stop for a breather five times on the way back due to a combination of Cecil's breathing and the crippling tightness and height of Stef's heels slowing him down. But damn her if the old bastard doesn't seem to be enjoying every second.

Shame the same can't be said for her shoes.

Stef is horrified when he returns them to her. There isn't a chance they'll fit her now, and never mind the scuffs to the heels, have them beyond repair. "You'll buy me a new pair. No, make it *two* pair. You may keep these."

She drops them negligently before stalking over to the stairs that lead to the front hall, grabbing the torch on her way. Still slopping along in Cecil's shoes, she tiptoes up the stairs in case Liam's lurking in the main hall. She only slips out of the brogues when she's right beside the secret panel.

That Cecil has to remove her shoes to put his back on has her smiling inwardly. He's a right demon for pain, just as Eadie warned her.

Stef has always prided herself on her hearing, but is surprised to see Cecil put his finger to his lips after straightening from putting his shoes back on. He takes the torch from her and clicks it off, leaving them to stand in the dark. At first Stef doesn't hear anything other than their combined breathing, but then she does.

How are they supposed to get back into the hall with someone lurking out there? Whoever it is, is methodically working their way around the hall, knocking on the walls, waiting and then continuing on, marking it firmly as Liam.

He's getting ever closer to their hiding spot, meaning it's only a matter of time before they're discovered. She's getting fidgety when she hears a loud bong from further away in the house. This is followed by a gasp of exasperation from frighteningly close by, before they hear footsteps retreating and a door slamming on the other side of the hall.

"Come on, my dear, we'll need to motor if we want to get free and clear."

Luckily for Stef, Cecil's idea of motoring is a brisk walk for her. However, on reaching the stairs, she flies up them two at a time to get to her room as quickly as she can. One hand on the bannister, the other hard across her stomach to keep the gold tile in place. No way can Liam catch sight of her barefoot and wearing only a leather corset and a fur-lined cloak.

She'd only realised she'd left her dress in the Folly when they reached the cellar and she was stuffed if she was going all the way back to get it.

No, she'll use it as an excuse to get Cecil to take her back there tomorrow. And this time, she's taking note of where it is that he pushes to release the panel in the hallway. Heaven only knows how many other floor tiles are gold like the one now sitting under a mountain of make-up in her toiletries caddy.

Stef pokes the perfectly rounded mound of gelatinous goo that sits proudly in the middle of her plate. No food she's aware of is this pink, naturally. Or this wobbly. "What is it?"

"Salmon mousse."

Cecil sucks a glob of the stuff off his fork before it can splatter back down onto his plate like several before. It's all Stef can do not to gag. The only upside to all of this is that Liam is as unimpressed with their starter as she is. After moving the parsley garnish a few times, he drops his cutlery with a clatter and pushes his plate to the side as far away as he can. The three of them clustered around the head of a table that's over twenty feet in length, this is a good long way.

"Oh, that's a shame. I'm allergic." Stef puts on her best disappointed expression, hoping she won't be pushed too much on what her allergy is. She doubts an allergy to food that resembles a pimply arse cheek is a real thing.

"So, Liam, how long will we have the *pleasure* of your company?" Cecil sits with a forkful of 'bum' precariously poised, waiting for his nephew to answer.

Rather than looking at his uncle, Liam gazes at Stef, raises an eyebrow and says, "I'm not so sure *this time*."

Stef stares back just as hard, giving no measure.

What does he mean this time? Does he always

pop up when his uncle has visitors? Is she the reason he's staying?

This would all be so much easier if he was pug-ugly. As it is, she's not sure if she's checking to see what he's up to, or simply because he's easy on the eye. She wouldn't go so far as to call him devastatingly handsome but, boy-oh-boy, he does do something for her. Shame he's off limits, in a big way.

Much to Stef and Liam's delight, the main course is a Beef Wellington that's firm to the bite without being tough. It's accompanied by vegetables that haven't had any colour boiled out of them; that the gravy isn't lumpy like her mum's is also a plus in Stef's eyes.

She's seen firsthand what's on offer in the pudding department in these big country places and wants an iron-clad excuse to get out of it. She stuffs herself with the main until her corset is ready to give at the seams, anything to prove her point of being full to bursting.

On seeing a chocolate gateau placed on the table in front of her, she could kick herself. Little wonder Liam hadn't hoovered his way through the main. If she was to swallow even the smallest sliver, she'd bring it all back. Not a good look.

There isn't another word out of Cecil as he ploughs his way through a slab of gateau that the size of your average house brick.

Liam then swallows another huge mouthful and taunts her further by licking his spoon. "Not hungry?"

Oh, she's hungry alright.

But he'll keep.

4

Stef thinks back over the evening while luxuriates in an enormous claw-foot tub that's just short of being Olympic in length, if not depth. Despite increasingly pointed comments from Cecil, Liam had proved as tenacious as cat fur on black pants when it came to refusing to leave her and the old chap alone.

It's this that sees her now relaxing in a hot bath before it's even gone nine pm, which is just as well as Cecil hadn't been up for anything too strenuous. He'd gone into what amounted to a food coma after polishing off most of the gateau.

The old geezer must have hollow legs.

She's working on how to get to and from the Folly without being caught by Liam for the umpteenth time when there's movement in her bedroom. Stef smiles broadly. Could it be Cecil isn't as tired as he'd seemed after all? Shame she's not at her dominant best lying as she is under a mountain of bubbles.

Even starkers would be better than this.

Stef eases herself out of the water and stands in the tub until the bulk of the bubbles have sluiced down her body. Clambering over the side, she grabs one of the enormous fluffy towels stacked on a chair at the end of the bath and dries herself rapidly and efficiently. She thinks for mere seconds before dropping the towel in the laundry hamper, swinging the door wide and striding out into her bedroom.

That's weird, there's no-one here. Now.

A quick scan of her belongings is enough to know they're not as they were before she took her bath. How long had whoever it was been rummaging about before she was aware of them?

She doubts it was Cecil as he'd have no reason to sneak about like a thief. Or more likely, he'd want to be caught doing so and thus earn himself a good spanking.

No, there's only one person it could have been. And damn if she isn't a little disappointed he's no longer here. Thank god her make-up bag with its golden secret had been in the bathroom with her. If it wasn't, she'd be back to being as poor as she had been on arrival.

It means one thing though, if she's retrieving more tiles, she'll need to find a bang-up hiding spot. But first she needs to get her mitts on the tiles and that'll involve a lot of hard work. Shame she hadn't thought to pack a boiler suit.

Stef stands in the middle of her room deep in thought. "I wonder?" The room doesn't answer back. That doesn't stop her striding over to the large coffin of a chest tucked into one corner of the room. She twists the key in the lock and lifts the lid and is immediately assailed by a cloud of camphor. One plus is that it's toxic enough to ensure any clothes in there will be in good shape.

She's been hoping for men's clothes. Far more practical for prising the gold tiles free in the Folly, lugging them out through the house and burying them for collection later. What she finds is almost as good. There are at least half a dozen riding habits in there, all ancient. Fortunately, they're serviceable and, more importantly, appear big enough that she won't have buttons popping at the first sign of exertion. Even better is they're all in dark jewel colours, perfect for skulking around the hallways of a pile like this.

Quarter of an hour later and she's ready. Not just a habit, but also riding boots, with a crop that fits snuggly in a pocket on the side of one boot. She decides against wearing one of the veiled hats. Instead she pulls her hair back in a solid plait that hangs down the middle of her back and well out of the way.

Then she waits.

And waits some more.

She's unsure which room Liam is in, if he actually has a room, or if he simply spends his time lurking in the hallway trying to catch someone at something. Her bedroom light switched off, she's able to tell the lights in the hallway are still burning bright. This will make it impossible to sneak around without that bastard Liam spotting her.

Turning, she leans her back against the bedroom door and allows the dark to close in around her. After shutting her eyes, she wills herself to think through the problem. What would her dad do? Hmmm, he'd probably jam a screwdriver into the nearest power point in hopes of shorting the lights in the entire place. Best not.

Only on opening her eyes does Stef see what she would otherwise have missed. It makes sense though. If there's one secret passage in a place this size, there are bound to be more. After pushing away from the door, she stalks across her room. Not once does she take her eye off the slivers of light that show another exit from her room. Is this how Liam got into her room earlier and left without her hearing her door opening and shutting?

Does she risk running into him back here as much as in the main hall itself?

Stef pushes the middle of the panel.

Nothing, apart from the light sneaking its way through the slits, fading until it's gone altogether.

Turning on her bedside lamp, Stef runs her hands over the wall in search of any protuberances; she pushes, prods, attempts to slide and generally gives the wall a good old grope.

Nothing.

Stef gazes down at her bedside lamp and then at the wall sconce that's right above it, she wonders. It makes no sense having two lights that close to each other. It's far too Agatha Christie, surely? She grasps the brass upright that's been fashioned to resemble a candle, and uses it as though pulling a pint of beer.

Nothing.

She twists the brass candle first one way and then the other and is finally rewarded with the faintest of clicks. This time when she pushes on the centre of the panel, it opens smoothly without so much as a whisper. No wonder she hadn't noticed him sneaking into her room.

Only a couple of steps into the space and her worry about her boots making too much noise are allayed. While the carpet is undoubtedly old and threadbare underfoot, it'll still muffle her steps perfectly. She gropes around in the dark until her hand falls on what she'd hoped. A small torch, hopefully with batteries that aren't flat because who knows when this one was last used. She's thinking Liam would surely have brought his own with him.

Phew. While small and not particularly bright, the torch will at least stop her from falling arse over tea kettle. It will also allow her to pinpoint any panels she can use to access other parts of the house.

She's not gone more than twenty feet when she hears noise off to her left. She switches off the torch without pause and stands stock still. Hardly breathing, she waits for her eyes to adjust to the pitch black. Just as back in her room, she can eventually make out the slivers of light that outline the panel.

However, this panel is different. This panel has peep holes, although none of them are at eye level. Nope, if she's looking through them, she'll need to hunker down. Down on her hands and knees while gussied up in a Victorian riding habit isn't easy, but she manages it without falling over or dropping the torch.

Unfortunately, what she sees on peeking through the small, round hole has the torch dropping from her nerveless fingers. The sound of it hitting the carpeted floor, although soft, is enough to have him swinging away from the bathroom sink and staring hard in her direction. Holy hell, he's a big boy. Especially from this angle and with him being naked and all.

It takes a second for Stef's addled brain to realise the reason he's getting bigger is that he's getting closer. Her head pulled back to give herself some space to think, she gives it a shake to clear it of erotic thoughts involving Liam as naked as he is now. *Bloody hell. What if he knows how to open the panel?*

A flustered grope around her feet, and Stef's hand lands on the torch. She flicks it on, trusting he won't see the light through peep hole, before swinging it wildly around. She's needs something to jam the door shut with, apart from herself, that is.

She slides a wooden peg into place seconds before Liam pushes against the panel, hard. "I know you're in there," he hisses through the gap between the panel and the wall. "And when I get hold of you."

He doesn't continue, instead putting his efforts into getting the panel to move, and causing the peg to groan as much as Liam himself. Stef's not waiting to find out if the peg's got dry rot or even the wet kind. After struggling to her feet, she takes off down the passage away from her bedroom. She's keeping as quiet as she can in hopes he won't know which direction she's gone in.

Her natural reaction was to head back to the safety of her bedroom, which is exactly why she's now flying in the other direction. She turns at random as she comes to each intersection, hoping to throw him off the scent.

She's lost count of how many corners she's turned and staircases she's gone up and down when she's dismayed to hear movement nearby. She accelerates, glad all those years spent standing behind bars have given her leg muscles with more power than most women. It's something she's using to her advantage.

After five more minutes of concerted twisting and turning, she again fights instinct, and stops and listens hard. There's still noise coming from the behind her, but it's definitely fainter than before. *Excellent.*

She races off again, and, after taking a couple more corners, chooses a panel at random and slides the pegs holding it in place quietly to the side.

She repeats the process with half a dozen more panels before missing a couple and then exiting into the library. At least it is if the mountains of books are any indicator. Even better is that it shows her to be on the ground floor, with French doors opening onto a patio. She opens these wide, making sure they stay open, and then scarpers in the other direction.

She inches the door to the hall open in case Mr Well Hung is lurking out there.

Finally, she's in luck. The hallway is empty and, more importantly, dark.

Even better is that the library is on the side of the foyer with the secret passage to the basement.

A couple of quick breaths to steady herself and Stef strides out into the brightly lit foyer. She grabs the wall sconce beside the panel, twists it, and disappears through the gap. It swings closed behind her a second later. Only then does she breathe.

Any luck and she's left Liam tripping around in the passages, or even searching for her outside. Either way he will have missed her disappearing act.

She isn't taking any chances. She locks the panel in place and grabs the larger torch and pocketing the smaller one. Sure, her dad had never actually taken her on a job, but she'd overhead enough planning sessions when she was little for some basics to stick.

Stef stuffs the tile into the pocket of her riding habit, pleased it's large enough. Without her corset on it's the safest place to carry it. She can hardly stroll through the main part of the house holding what ostensibly looks to be a floor tile.

She's located half a dozen more by walking around the space in bare feet, although only prising this one free. Safer to leave them where they are than risk running into Liam while weighted down like a pack horse.

There's no time to waste. She skips down the stairs and takes off along the passage toward the house, her way lit by the large torch. As tempting as it had been to turn the lights on, she'd decided against this in favour of subterfuge. Last thing she needs is for Liam to stumble upon the subterranean cavern because it's lit up like Christmas.

Only when the passage starts to angle up does she slow her pace. She even goes so far as to turn the torch off and creep along the last few feet by feel only. She knows from having seen the floor of the passage in electric light that there's nothing for her to trip over.

Surprise then, when on taking another step forward, the toe of her boot catches on something, sending her flying forward into the dark.

Damn, this is going to hurt.

It's not the floor of the passage she's tripped over. Rather, it's a solid mountain of flesh, with a quick grope letting her know it's definitely not Cecil. The other discovery is that Liam didn't bother getting dressed before starting his pursuit of her.

5

If there's one thing Stef's old man has taught her, it's how to take care of herself. A skill that's helped her eject many a drunken punter after closing hours, now comes in handy. It allows her to free herself from Liam's grip, likely breaking one of his fingers in the process.

Her stumbling to her feet has the heel of one of her riding boots in contact with a bit of him not used to being treated like a stirrup. She doesn't bother fighting the grin at his shouted oath.

She's turned the corner and has started up the stairs when she hears enough movement behind her to know he's already on his feet. Impressive, but not fast enough to catch her before she's unlocked the panel, raced across the foyer, and shot up the stairs as though the coppers are on her tail.

She isn't heading for her own room. She'd be bonkers to do that. Instead she nips around the corner and opens the first door she comes across, closing herself into the darkness seconds later.

The room doesn't remain dark for long.

She's still turning the key in the lock when a light across the room flares into life. Cecil is struggling to sit up in bed and blinking in an effort to wake properly. He's not sleepy for long when he takes in her outfit.

The familiar gleam showing in his eye, Stef decides to make the best of a bad situation. She retrieves the whip from its pocket on the side of her boot and whacks it against the leather for good measure. It's then she realises that somewhere between her encounter with Liam and reaching the safety of Cecil's bedroom, she's lost the second blasted tile. Damn it, now she really needs to whip out her frustrations.

Lucky for her that Cecil enjoys nothing better.

. . .

Breakfast the next morning is a quiet affair with no sign of Liam, although a set of used dishes and a half-empty cup of coffee indicate he's eaten earlier.

"Do you have to stand there like that?"

Stef feels like a right plonker sitting at the over-sized table on her own, while Cecil stands, eating his bacon and eggs at the side board. It wasn't as though she'd whacked the old codger's flabby arse that hard. Nothing he'd said he couldn't handle, at any rate.

"My dear, you simply don't know your own strength." Cecil's tone is one of admiration.

"Sit!" Stef nods toward the chair at the head of the table.

"But," Cecil pauses with a fork-full of scrambled egg, ready to shove it into his mouth.

"Now!"

Stef's tone brooks no argument and is authoritative enough that he swallows hard, before putting his fork and uneaten egg back down on the plate. He then gathers everything up and walks meekly to take his place at the table. He isn't able to stop a hiss of pain when his bum hits the softly upholstered carver chair.

Surely I didn't hit him that hard?

She's having second thoughts on the effort she'd put in when Cecil interrupts her thoughts.

"I thought we could take another gander at the Folly this afternoon."

Hah, so much for him being in pain or, more to the point, in too much pain to be uninterested in a further paddling. Stef isn't keen on visiting the shrine to B&D with the old bloke in tow any time soon. While on the quest for tiles the night before, she'd had a chance to check out the *toys* there and didn't want a bar of them. If she was to wield half the items in that room, Cecil would be Cecilia quicker than you could say *castration* three times in a row.

Stef stands so abruptly that her chair is thrown backward clattering to the floor. She leans over the table, towering over him. In a low voice, full of as much menace as she can rustle up, she growls at him. "How dare you tell me what to do?"

Actually he hadn't, but close enough for her purposes. "I'm leaving."

She follows through on her promise by storming out of the room as dramatically as she can without risking laughter. Her own. Shame her exit is ruined when she collides with Liam just outside the door, hard enough that he sends her back a couple of steps.

"You going somewhere?"

"Home. I'll need a ride to the station."

"I'm busy!" Liam's response is at abrupt as her request has been, with his broad smile irritating in the extreme.

Stef doesn't say a thing, instead swinging back to face Cecil and spearing him with a glance that has him squirming.

"Afraid I'm not able to, my dear. If the local constabulary catch me behind the wheel, there'll be the devil to pay."

"That's if he doesn't end up in ditch first," says Liam.

"Grrrrrr." Stef's unable to stop vocalising her disapproval. She's stuffed if she's staying here with Liam in residence. Better to come back another time when she'll be free and clear to grab as many tiles as she can.

But how am I supposed to get to the train station? It's too far to walk.

The solution comes to her when she's stomping her way up to her room. It won't be the easiest option, although worth it even if she won't be around to see the expression on Liam's face. Watch him try to smile then.

In the end, the easiest part of her departure is hot-wiring the Land Rover. Just as well, because after finding the heap of junk and lugging her suitcase down from her room, she's ready to drop.

Any exhaustion on her part falls away as she sweeps past the front doors of the house and sees Liam exploding out of the front doors. While the Land Rover isn't the fastest vehicle around, it's thankfully faster than Liam's ground-devouring strides. He then gives up and runs as fast in the other direction. This has her abandoning her plan to only use the Land Rover to get as far as the train station.

There's only one reason he's running as fast as he is, and that's because there's another vehicle on the property. Not that she noticed one parked in the garage.

"Come on ya bucket of bolts!" Stef stomps her foot down on the accelerator as hard as she can, thankful she's wearing the riding boots rather than her stilettos. The Land Rover lurches forward, albeit sluggishly, increasing in speed ever so slowly until she's going a respectable 50 miles an hour when she passes the station. As to where she goes from here, she relies on instinct. It's always served her well in the past, so hopefully it'll do so again.

Stef's feeling good about her choices of left and right turns when Liam's disembodied voice fills the cab and she nearly steers off the road.

"You can run missy, but you can't hide."

"Hah! Just watch me," shouts Stef, even if she understands he can't hear her. Nor is she picking up the mic and responding as he's probably expecting.

"Do you know what I'll do when I catch up with you?"

Stef's imagining all sorts of bad things when his rich chuckle rumbles out of the speaker and touches her in places it has no right.

"Bloody 'ell." Stef snaps the radio off; worried she'll have an accident, or climax, if she keeps listening to him.

She can't help but sigh with relief when she stumbles upon the A40. After that it's plain sailing into London, with her tension easing enough she's able to hum a tune to herself. That is, until she spots a motorbike in her rearview mirror. It's not the first time she's seen it but it's not gaining on her, just staying half a dozen car lengths behind her. Despite her plan being to head straight to Chiswick, that's so not happening. If it is Liam on the motorbike, there's not a chance she wants to lead him there.

After checking to see if she isn't just being paranoid, Stef takes four right-hand turns in a row and, sure enough, the motorbike is still showing in the rear-view mirror.

Blast him.

What starts out as a small smile soon morphs into a full-on grin. Let's see how he likes it when she leads him on a merry chase through the East End. It's an area where she knows every shortcut and alley, and where there's also a particular builder's yard.

It's one that she'll be able to sail straight through, but he won't. Well, not if her Uncle Reggie has anything to say about it. She's got her fingers crossed he's actually there and not out on some 'job' with her dad.

Stef swings the Land Rover around another corner and into what appears to be a dead-end alley, pulling to a stop just short of the large gates that span the road.

Three short, followed by three long, beeps on the horn have these swinging open, allowing her to drive straight in. She doesn't stop, only slows enough that she can wind the window down and yell out

"I'm being followed by a geezer on a motorbike. Stall him as long as you can!"

On receiving a nod of understanding from her Uncle, Stef accelerates across the yard and through the double gates on the other side. These slam shut not long after her exit. Rather than heading straight for Chiswick, she takes the most convoluted route she can, something made difficult by the lack of agility on the part of the Land Rover.

It takes an hour to get to Eadie's place. Much as she'd like to do nothing more than to put her feet up and have a cuppa, her new plan doesn't give her time.

"Hey Eadie, flying visit!" Stef dumps her bag in the hallway and bursts into the sitting room.

"Good lord, what happened? Why are you home early?"

"This!"

Stef sucks in her stomach and is rewarded when the tile drops out the bottom of her corset, landing with a bounce on the plush carpet.

"What on earth?" Eadie holds her hand out.

"Careful, it's bleeding 'eavy." Stef places it carefully in Eadie's lap to avoid the old girl having to take the weight.

"Gold?" Eadie's expression now matches that of Stef when she'd first discovered the tile in the Folly.

"Solid! I think."

"But where on earth did you find it?"

"Arthur's Folly."

Stef explains how she'd come to discover the tile and the fact it was only one of many. "Liam will know about it by now. I dropped one by accident in the secret passage."

"He may know about the one you dropped but you can be sure he doesn't know about the rest."

"Why'd ya say that?"

"Because if he knew, they wouldn't still be grappling with the crippling death duties Arthur's unfortunate death encumbered them with.

"Unfortunate?"

"Erotic asphyxiation," says Eadie, absently. "He was a gasper of the extreme variety. Ginny

Roberts was never the same after. Arthur hated using his safe word, so it was always touch-and-go between his coming and accidentally going. His timing and hers were off something chronic that day. By the time the doctor arrived, there was nothing for him to do but sign the death certificate."

"That's how the place got its name, isn't it?"

"Yes, Liam hates it, but the name has stuck with a select few."

Stef retrieves the tile from Eadie's lap. "Damn, this means I'll have to take this back, doesn't it?"

"Are you mad? If this gold comes from where I think it does, then one missing tile will be neither here nor there. No, you keep that as a little nest egg and tell Cecil about the rest."

"Bugger. I'd better get moving then. Lean forward."

Eadie doesn't hesitate to comply and Stef drops the tile safely behind the pillow at the back of the old lady's chair. She plumps the pillow and helps her mentor settle back down again. "Safe as 'ouses back there. I'll deal with it when I get back."

. . .

The return trip to Ryder Hall is accomplished relatively quickly. Not because of the performance of the rusty Land Rover, but more to Stef knowing where she's actually going. There also no need to take evasive action to shake Liam and she's certainly sitting more comfortably without a gold tile shoved down her underwear.

As the miles disappear, she rehearses her return. Going through every argument, complaint and bitch that Liam can come up with. She's not worried about Cecil. Him she can settle with a well-aimed glare.

What a disappointment then to swing into the garage without encountering an irate Liam. To be able to lug her suitcase back up to her room without so much as a peep out of anyone. She then searches the house for Cecil, finding him in his favourite spot for this time of day; in the conservatory with a glass of whisky.

On seeing her, Cecil goes from being hunched over his drink, to sitting up straight and smiling broadly. "You came back!"

"Someone's gotta keep you in line!"

Stef helps herself to a drink—lord knows she needs one—before taking the seat next to Cecil. "Where's Liam?" Stef knows it's only a matter of time before he pops up behind a palm.

"Not sure. Haven't seen him all day."

"He's not here?"

"No."

Stef slugs her drink back, slams her glass down on the small cane table and then leans over and takes Cecil's drink away from him. She puts it next to her empty.

"Come on, I've got something to show you and you need to see it before Liam's back."

6

They're not even halfway to the Folly when Stef loses patience. At this rate the bloody gold will have been reclaimed by the earth by the time they sodding get there.

She squeezes past Cecil, stops in her tracks, and hunkers down. "Get on!"

"What? I can't ride you like a brood mare."

"If you don't get on, I'm turning around and I'm leaving. For good!"

The second part of their journey goes a lot faster, although Stef rips strips off Cecil when he gleefully calls out "Tallyho". She's not reversing their roles that much.

Only once he's settled on the fainting couch in the Folly does Stef get down on her hands and knees and peel the carpet back. There's no reaction from the old gent, proving again whoever painted the gold tiles to imitate terracotta did a bang-up job.

"Give me a second." A nipple clamp grabbed off a nearby table and Stef can't help but laugh at the look of hope from Cecil. "Think you're gonna like what I'm about to show ya a lot more than that."

Working away at the grout surrounding the tile she's found purely by feel, Stef's aware of Cecil leaning forward, his elbows on his knees, his attention firmly on her hands. His gasp when she works the tile free is exactly as hers had been when she'd found both the first and second.

She hands it to him and can tell he's as surprised by the weight as she had been.

"Gold?"

"Yep. And probably enough to deal to some death duties plus change for a holiday."

Stef hopes there's enough left for a holiday as she doesn't want to spend her tile on anything like that. No, she'd like to put it toward a small flat. She's lived in cramped quarters most of her life, a space she can call her own is something she covets. A place where the landlord can't put the rent up at a moment's notice or decide he's evicting her because she's a week behind on it. A haven.

"I wonder if Liam knows about this," says Cecil.

"If he didn't before, he will now."

At least Stef thinks he knows. She hadn't even bothered to check the floor of the passage for the second tile, sure that Liam would have grabbed it soon after she'd lost it.

"Wait here!"

Stef doesn't want to be slowed down by Cecil. All she wants is to run to the other end of the passage, scramble around on the floor, and then race back. Indeed, she doesn't even wait for him to acknowledge her comment before legging it, making good time without an aging lord draped over her like a cheap coat.

Now that she knows what she's after, it makes finding the tile easier. Maybe having landed terracotta-side up is why Liam hadn't spotted it. If it'd landed other side up, he'd have seen it in a heartbeat. Fortunately the passage had only been lit with the light borrowed from the cellar area.

She's about to pick up the tile when she's overcome by a foreboding. It's one that sees her leaving it where it is and returning to the Folly at belting speed. She'll be able to try out for the Olympics at this rate. The light switch at the top of the stairs flicked off, she plunges the passage behind her into a Stygian marathon for anyone on her tail.

She listens carefully, even pausing her breathing. Nope, she can't hear any movement, although that's not to say there isn't anyone behind her.

"Is there a key to this lock?" Stef taps the door quietly for emphasis so he knows which lock she's talking about.

Cecil takes a moment to answer, engaged as he is in levering another tile free of the floor.

"Yes, on a hook behind the curtain."

Then he's straight back to beavering away on saving his estate from taxes.

Stef locks the door and then, for good measure, draws the deep red velvet curtain across it. This ensures any light from inside the Folly won't be seen out in the passage. There only remains one problem. If Liam does track them down here, and he's already proven he knows where the passage is, they're trapped like rats. It's not a feeling she likes.

Quarter of an hour passes before Stef allows Cecil to move again. Enough time that

Liam would have been able to reach the Folly, even if he'd had to crawl in the dark on all fours. Then it's all go, with both of them working away in different areas of the Folly.

After digging up a dozen tiles between them, they notice a pattern emerging. This makes finding more tiles a lot easier although the digging part remains as painful as ever. If she'd thought this through, they'd have come here armed with appropriate tools. But she'd been concentrating on getting here before Liam got back.

It's while Cecil is taking another breather on the fainting couch that Stef asks about something that's been bugging her. "Is there another way out of this place?"

"Apparently. Although I've never worked out where it is."

"Right, you keep digging, I'll work out how we can get out of here without the risk of running into your nephew."

To a background of tapping and scraping, Stef examines every inch of the place. Twice. Without finding so much as a loose bit of wooden trim. "Shit!"

"Nothing?"

"No. I'm damned if I can see another way out of this place."

"Maybe a closer look at the altar?"

Although not consciously, Stef finally admits to herself she's been avoiding this centrepiece of the room. Chances are, with it being made out of solid marble and all, there won't be any panels sliding to the side any time soon.

Stepping up onto the plinth, she circles it, taking in the various manacles and chains that are bolted to its sides. There's not the slightest gap anywhere that she can see, even after her third lap of it. It's not until she slaps her hands down on top of it in frustration that the bleeding obvious becomes, well, obvious.

"It's hollow! And it sure as hell aint marble."

"Ah, yes. It's rococo. Marble's far too cold for old bones," says Cecil, glancing up from his scrabbling. Soon after he holds another tile triumphantly aloft and adds it to the mounting pile beside him.

Stef, who has no idea what he's on about, turns back toward the altar and pushes against it tentatively. Any hope that the whole thing will simply swivel to the side are quickly dashed. Now she knows it's made out of wood, she'll smash the bleeding thing if she has to.

But she might not have to. A proper examination of the chains dangling down either side of the altar has her spotting something. It's something she would have missed if she hadn't been specifically hunting for it.

"Bingo!"

Stef twists what seems like a length of chain and is rewarded when the whole altar slides backwards to reveal a stone staircase descending to lord knows where. The stench of mould and damp that wafts out, points to it not having been used in a good long time. Close to twenty-five years if what her dad was saying is true.

"You stay here and I'll go check this out." She grabs the larger of the two torches and, switching it on, aims it down into the dark. She's hoping beyond hope that there aren't too many creepy crawlies lurking down there. Thank goodness the riding boots will keep anything on the floor well away from her toes.

"Be careful, my dear."

Stef's so careful, she's just this side of crawling, taking her own good time to descend the steps. The passage at the bottom must be a lot deeper underground than the one leading from the house. Even better, when she reaches it she's pleased to see she's able to stand tall without the cobwebs hanging from the ceiling catching in her hair. It's also wide enough for two people to walk abreast without scraping the bricks that line it.

"Right. Let's see where you're gonna lead me to."

Stef starts out slowly, but when the floor of the passage changes from slippery bricks to fine gravel, she increases her pace knowing she won't slip on this. It still takes an eternity for the passage to start to slant upwards, letting her know she's getting closer to an exit. Hopefully one she's able to open.

Even expecting the end of the passage as she is, being faced with a solid wall of boards and battens comes as a surprise. That there are wooden pegs at regular intervals down the right-hand edge is a good sign, meaning it's unlikely to be locked from the other side. Question is, where will it open up to? Hopefully not straight into the living room of some worker's cottage, or the main bar of the local pub. She sure feels like she's walked far enough that she could even be on the outskirts of London.

Sliding the pegs out of their holes isn't as easy here as it had been with the panels in the house. It takes a good amount of jiggling before she's able to work each of them free. Not knowing what's on the other side, she's keeping the squeaking to a minimum. Even so, if there is someone on the other side they'll be standing on a chair by now. Or armed with a broom.

Finally the last peg gives up its hold and Stef puts it on the ground next to the others. Grabbing the torch, she points it towards the panel, grabs the handle, and, after flicking the torch off, pulls the whole thing toward her.

It moves a tiny bit, but then jams. She shakes her head to clear it of images of everyone in an unseen bar suddenly stopping with their pints, staring horrified at the wall and wondering if it's time to call it a night.

After turning the torch back on, Stef once again points it at the wall. She must have missed something for the panel to have moved as little as it did. She directs the torchlight first down one side and then other, there are no obstructions she can see. She sweeps it across the top, even running her hand along the edge of the panel in case there's a hidden mechanism.

Still nothing.

It's not until she shines the torch on the floor and checks it out it properly that she spots the problem. She stomps hard on the brick, trying to bed it down like those that surround it. All this does is send a shooting pain up her leg. It also has a loud boom reverberating through the passage.

Bugger. Shame she doesn't have a nipple clamp handy. For sure she'll have to dig the blasted brick free if she wants the panel to swing wide enough for her to squeeze through.

Her cussing and swearing does no good, but it does tamp down her level of frustration enough that she can think logically about the problem at hand. It's only when she goes to hang the torch back on the spike in the wall, that it all becomes clear.

She doesn't even have to try hard to remove the spike from the wall. This is down to it having been jammed in a gap in the oak upright rather than hammered in place. After that it's mere seconds' work to remove the brick and stack it to the side with the wooden pegs.

Once again she grabs hold of the wooden handle on the panel and turns the torch off.

This time when she pulls on the panel, it swings wide without so much as a squeak.

But, on seeing what's waiting for her on the other side, there's no way Stef can keep quiet. Anything but.

7

Liam sits there like he owns the place, a whisky in one hand while the other casually grips the trigger of the shotgun that's sitting across his lap.

After slugging the contents of the glass, he drops it beside his chair before hefting the shotgun up and swinging it in her direction. While this is bad, it's the black eye he's sporting that gives her pause. Looks like Reggie and his boys have been a little heavy-handed when it came to stalling him back at the builder's yard.

"What have you done with my Uncle?" he barks at her.

Staring down the double barrels, Stef sees red. "What the bleeding 'ell do you mean, what 'ave I done with 'im?"

Damn it, Eadie would give her a right bollocking if she could hear all these dropped H's they've worked so hard to rid her of.

"We can't afford another scandal like that my unfortunate father caused the family. I refuse to be the laughingstock of the county, again. So I'll ask again. What have you done with my Uncle?"

"I aint snuffed 'im, if that's what you was thinking."

The shotgun drops a little, but not so far that she wouldn't be knee-capped. In an effort to avoid any damage to her person at all, Stef adds "He was alive and kicking when I saw him half an 'our ago."

Liam leans to the side to peer around her into the darkness of the passage behind. "Where is he then?"

"Relax would ya." Stef nods at the shotgun for emphasis. "When I left 'im, he was on his hands and knees in the Folly. He was getting stuck in with a nipple-clamp like there was no tomorra. Happy as a choir boy receiving a private communion."

"He was what?!" yells Liam, surging to his feet and storming across the room to tower over her, the gun now a lot closer to her head than she'd like. "If you've harmed him in any way, you will pay dearly for it."

This is interesting. The bloke seems genuinely concerned about the welfare of his uncle. If he's simply holding out for his inheritance, surely he'd be happy to see the old codger popping his clogs. Perhaps just not from erotic asphyxiation given the family history.

Any further thoughts are scattered when he nudges her with the gun, forcing her to turn back down the passage and retrace her steps.

If she'd thought the trip out was a nightmare, being prodded in the back every time she much as slows on the return journey, isn't fun.

Finally, she's had enough. She stops dead, and reasonably sure she won't end up that way, swings toward him, shining the torch directly into his eyes and grits out. "If you bleeding nudge me with that sodding gun one more time, I'll take the bloody thing off ya and shove it where the sun don't shine. We clear!"

Only on receiving the slightest of nods in response does she storm off, leaving him to follow as best he can, given she's the one with the torch. Thankfully she doesn't get any more prompting of the steel kind before reaching the stairs to the Folly. She doesn't slow, instead climbing the stairs as rapidly as she can. If she can just make it through the gap and slide the altar back into place, she'll be home free.

Unfortunately, Liam's long legs once again work in his favour. She's unable to click the altar back into place before the barrel of the gun is slammed through the gap.

"Ah, I see you've brought company," says Cecil, who's once again taking a breather on the fainting couch. When she sees how many tiles are sitting under it, Stef's not surprised he's knackered. He's been busy.

The altar smashes back hard with the unholy racket having both Stef and Cecil covering their ears. Liam then stands tall on the plinth next to the altar, his gaze darting about wildly as though expecting to find his uncle tied up and tortured.

How very disappointing for him.

After slamming the gun down on top of the altar, he's at his uncle's side in seconds. "You're hurt?"

"Hurt? Why on earth would I be hurt?"

"Her!" spits Liam, over his shoulder. "That's her stock in trade, isn't it?"

Cecil gazes up at her, his face a picture of

guilt. "Stefanie, promise you won't take this the wrong way."

Stef's unable to stop, her hackles rising in readiness. A warning like this and she knows damn well she won't like what he's about to say. She's unable to stop herself from crossing her arms in readiness.

Cecil turns back at Liam. "Stefanie's a kitten."

"A kitten!" Both Liam and Stef explode at the same time.

While Liam is looking at her in disbelief, she's staring daggers at Cecil, her mind already whirring on him pretending to be in pain at breakfast only that morning. The crafty old bugger. No way will he need to pretend he's in pain after their next session.

That's if there is another session. And taking a peek at Liam, she doubts it.

"Hang on a goddam second." This has both men gaping at her. "Why on earth are you letting this pip squeak tell you what you can and can't do?"

"Pip squeak!" Liam draws himself up to his full height, showing he's anything but. "Has my uncle not explained to you that the estate actually passed to me on my father's death?"

"To you?" Even though she's addressed her question to Liam, she waits on Cecil to respond and is gob smacked when he nods.

"And one of the provisos to my uncle receiving his stipend from the estate is that he's not to indulge in the abominations he so enjoys."

"Oh my god, that's what the Smythe-Browns were using against you, isn't it?"

The old man nods briefly.

Blackmail aside, Cecil's addiction to pain must be something else. Enough to risk losing his home and income, all for the sake of a few stolen moments with someone like her. "Cecil, why didn't you say something?"

"And pass up the opportunity to use the Folly?" All that's missing from his response is the "Are you mad?" that remains hanging in the air.

"Hell yes if it stops this arsehole kicking you out."

"That's it. I will not be insulted in my own home. You!" He points at Stef to confirm she's about to get the old heave-ho, "Leave now. And no, you can't use the Land Rover. As far as I'm concerned you can walk to the damn station."

When she doesn't move fast enough for his

liking, he grabs her by the arm and frog marches her across the room, unlocks the door and shoves her through it.

"I'll help my uncle back to the main house. When we get there, I want you gone."

Knowing how slow Cecil moves, Stef wastes no time in scarpering, flicking the lights on at the top of the stairs. It's not that she's scared of Liam, but more that she's got things to do. Without the need to slow for Cecil or because she's walking by torchlight, Stef makes the most of the weak lightbulbs. They allow her to all but jogs to the other end of the passage. Let Liam think she's in awe of him.

The floor of the passage has started to slant upwards when she slows. She's now scanning every square inch of the floor from side to side in a sweeping motion.

"Bingo." She says quietly to herself before bending over to retrieve the second tile.

She'll be stuffed if she's handing this over to Liam now that she knows he's the one facing the crippling death duties. Maybe if he hadn't proven himself to be such a pain in the bum, she'd be feeling more benevolent. "I wonder?" she says into the quiet of the passage.

She doesn't bother waiting to find out, instead shooting up the stairs to the foyer and then not wasting a second in getting up to her bedroom. She's soon dressed in the Victorian riding habit of the night before and has shoved everything back in her suitcase.

Rather than lugging this downstairs, she drags it around the corner and dumps it in Cecil's room before hightailing it down the stairs and out the front door.

Hot wiring the motorbike isn't necessary, with the key still being in the ignition. She's only ridden one once before, but it's enough to see her already a good distance down the driveway before Liam explodes out the front door. Well, he did say not to take the Land Rover. He didn't say a damned thing about half-inching the motorbike.

Back at the house in Chiswick, Eadie looks up as Stef walks into the sitting room. "Where did you get the motorbike from?"

"Borrowed it off a friend."

"Oh yes, and who would that be?"

"Goes by the name of Liam." Stef's unable to stop her lip from curling in disgust.

"Arthur's boy?"

"That's him. Self-important bastard and the rightful owner of Ryder Hall."

It's not often Eadie is shocked, but Stef can see that she too has been unaware of this titbit, with her face writ large with disbelief. "And Cecil confirmed this?"

"Yep."

"This certainly changes things."

"How's that?"

"Well, for one thing, it's Liam who's got access to the money and not Cecil as we'd thought when Brenda and I suggested you strike up a friendship with him."

"Damn. I hadn't even thought about that. Just as well I got this then, isn't it?"

Stef again sucks in her tummy and the gold tile drops out the bottom of her corset. It then slides down the leg of the divided skirt, and lands with a thunk on the carpet.

"You got another one?"

"More than one. Last I saw Cecil had dug up at least a dozen or so."

"And Liam knows about them."

"Now there I can't help you."

. . .

The rest of the evening is spent in contemplation of where Stef should go from here. It would be a complete waste of time to flirt with Liam. She's well and truly blotted her copy book by borrowing first the Land Rover and then the motorbike.

"The easiest solution," Eadie pauses to take a large gulp of sherry, "is to wait until Cecil is back in town and simply ask him."

"And then what? There's no way I can go back there and just waltz in the front door like I own the place and grab 'em. I'd need a bleeding wheelbarrow."

"What about the other exit from the Folly?"

"Wouldn't have a darned clue where it was. I only saw the one room and with Liam sitting there with a shot gun, I didn't like to go any further."

"But it was an old building, you say?"

"Yeah, near derelict, if you ask me."

"Well, that's got to limit it. I'm sure Cecil can point you in the right direction if he wants to get his mitts on those gold tiles. At least before Liam stumbles upon them."

"Shhhh. Do you hear that?" Stef jumps up, getting her ear as close to the curtained front window as the couch will allow. Damn, she'd recognise the tappets doing their thing on that bucket of bolts anywhere. But how on earth did Liam find her here? It wasn't like he was on her tail when she left the property and she definitely didn't see him on the trip to London.

"Stef, the tiles!" Eadie hisses from behind her, breaking her out of her reverie.

A couple of giant strides and Stef scoops them up off the coffee table. Eadie tilts forward as far as her arthritis allows and the tiles disappear down the back of the old lady's chair.

No sooner has the pillow been plumped than there's an urgent banging at the front door.

"Show time!" says Stef, shaking the tension out of her shoulders before bending over and grabbing the horse whip out of the pocket on the side of her boot.

8

Stef forces herself to walk to the front door, the riding crop at the ready to do some damage to Liam if he decides to forgo manners. It's almost a disappointment, when on opening it she has to adjust her line of sight down about a foot.

"Ooooh, I've been bad. So very, very bad," says Cecil, his look of contrition having a practiced air about it.

Stef stares over the top of his head, but can't see any sign of Liam. "Did you drive here by yourself?" A quick check of the Land Rover shows it to be in the same shape as last time she'd seen it. "Without crashing?"

Cecil skips past her and disappears into the front room without answering, leaving her to shut the front door and follow him. There's a problem, though. A very large boot is in the way, stopping the door from closing. Unfortunately, it's attached to Liam.

"Not so fast... Kitten."

That he grins broadly after calling her this has Stef lifting her arm. She's ready to give him a right walloping, but he's too fast. He grabs her by the wrist and gently takes the riding crop off her. He then uses it to point her in the direction of the sitting room as though he's the host and she's the guest. *Bloody cheek.*

Stef throws herself down on the couch, making sure to hog as much space as she can in hopes Liam will remain standing. No such luck. He starts lowering himself ever so slowly and Stef knows if she doesn't move she'll end up with the smart arse sitting on her lap. *Never a hat pin handy when you need one.*

She's only just settled herself as far from Liam as possible, when Eadie speaks.

"Stef, would you be so good as to ask Bert to rustle up a pot of tea for us and maybe a few biscuits?"

"Ah, yeah. Sure." Stef clambers to her feet, unable to keep the puzzlement off her face. Eadie drinking tea after ten in the morning isn't something she's seen since living here.

What is she up to?

Something smells fishy, Stef races through to the kitchen, tosses the request for a cuppa in Bert's direction and is back in no time at all. But, long enough for Liam to be sitting smack bang in the middle of the blasted couch.

Much as she'd like to use his own tactic on him, she doubts he'd move and she does not want to end up on his lap. Instead she grabs the hoop back chair that sits at the small escritoire in the corner of the room. She drags it over next to the coffee table, swings it around and straddles it.

On hearing her elderly mentor's sharp intake of breath, Stef laughs. "Relax would ya, Eadie? It's a split skirt." Stef flaps the material, showing she's not about to flash her knickers to anyone. She leans forward, props her chin on the hoop of the chair and looks at the other two. "So, who the 'ell's telling me what the bleeding hell is going on?"

"We always knew the gold was somewhere on the estate, but we couldn't find it." Liam has the nerve to seem peeved that she's found it rather than him.

"Yes, well." Cecil scouts around for the right

words. "The sticking point is that it's not exactly ours."

"Then who does it belong to?" Again Stef turns to each of them, but it's Eadie who is busting to tell her. "Go on."

"It was never reported in the papers, but the rumours were rife."

"And," says Stef, prompting her to continue, because so far she's no further ahead in understanding what's going on than she was five minutes ago.

Cecil coughs to gain her attention. "Arthur used to drink at the Oakley pub. Supposedly they used to pop in there for a quick pint when they got sick of being holed up at the farmhouse."

Stef's had enough. "Who's they? What didn't the papers report? Where the 'ell is Oakley?"

Cecil and Eadie start talking over the top of each other in an effort to give her as much information as they can, as quickly as possible. They only stop when Liam whistles loudly enough to have the figurines in the china cabinet rattling.

With everyone's full attention, he speaks. "Ryder Hall is near Oakley. Also near Oakley is

Leatherslade Farm, where the robbers holed up after they'd committed the greatest train robbery of all time. My father, Arthur, used to like to pop down to the pub at Oakley for a quick one and apparently got talking to one of the gang there. He bought the chap enough drinks that he let slip about some gold that hadn't been on the manifesto. Gold that they'd had a devil of a job getting back to the farm because it weighed a ton. To this day there's never been any mention of missing gold and the police have never reported its recovery."

"So you think Arthur helped 'imself when the crims were all locked up or in South America."

"We do," says Liam. "In fact we know he did, because he told me himself."

"Just not where it was," adds Cecil.

"So that's why he bought Leatherslade Farm when the crown auctioned it off," says Eadie. She stares up at the ceiling before continuing. "It made no sense at the time, and Arthur was always cagey as to why he'd acquired it."

"We all thought he was barking," says Cecil. "He paid through the nose for the place."

"But what my Uncle and I would like to

know is what *you two* are doing about it?" Liam glances first at Eadie and then at Stef.

"From the sound of things, we've got a lot of work to do." Eadie's eyes are alight with excitement and if her hands weren't so crippled with arthritis, Stef knows she'd be rubbing them together. As it is, she gets a puzzled look from Liam.

"What my nephew would like to know is, will you go to the authorities?"

Eadie snorts, as is her way. "And do what? Report finding some gold that isn't missing?"

"Stuffed if I'll be dobbing you in. I'll need a finder's fee though," says Stef.

From the sound of things, there's a lot more gold than the few tiles she and Cecil have managed to dig up. Her two tiles are chicken feed compared to what could be on offer.

"One percent. No more." Liam leans back and crosses his arms, telling her it's not open to negotiation.

Naïve sod. Stef smiles broadly and is rewarded when he relaxes, thinking she's agreeing to this paltry cut. Like hell she is. If it wasn't for her, they'd still be searching for the sodding gold. There's also the fact she's more than likely already got that percentage stuffed down the back of Eadie's chair.

Her casually uttered "Ten percent and not a penny less," has him tense enough you could bounce pennies off him. Stef wishes she had a few handy, just to test her theory out.

Liam thrusts himself forward to the edge on the couch, his body angled in her direction in a manner that's just shy of threatening. "That's robbery!"

"No, that's what your dad did. Even though he didn't flog the gold 'imself, he still 'elped 'imself when no one was about. Mates of my dad know people who are still inside for that job. Trust me, they won't be pleased to find out your dad helped himself to their hard-earned brass." This is actually a wild summation on Stef's part, but something her dad had said in the car made her think she isn't too far off the mark.

"Hard-earned brass?" Liam has the nerve to look indignant, conveniently forgetting the fact his dad hadn't earned it either.

"How about five percent?" says Cecil, his voice hopeful. Whether this is of her accepting the offer or avoiding a full-on stoush, who knows.

Five percent is actually what Stef's been after all along, but she's seen her mum haggling over the price of fish down the market enough to know how it's done. Gold, fish, goldfish, didn't matter what it was, premise was the same. Start high.

"Deal." Stef thrusts her hand in Cecil's direction, both because he's the closer of the two and she doesn't trust Liam not to crush her hand in spite.

"Fine, five percent," agrees Liam, "but you get to help us dig it up."

And so it is, Stef finds herself down on her hands and knees in the Folly being whipped into shape by Liam. He's proving himself to be quite the drill sergeant. Stef squints at yet another ripped and torn fingernail. Damn it, it was the last one still intact. She should have pushed for ten percent. Cecil is still up in town with Eadie, leaving her and Liam to do the heavy lifting. The older pair is working on how to convert the tiles into cold hard cash and more importantly where that should go.

Stef knows Brenda has a Swiss bank account and thinks that's what she'll do with her cut. Far enough away that her mum and dad won't be constantly hitting her up for loans that never get repaid, but close enough she can buy that place of her own. Stef holds up yet another tile and flips it over to reveal the gold showing on the underside. A penthouse would be nice.

A noise from the centre of the room has Stef glancing up to see Liam stagger out of the stairs usually hidden under the altar. The boilersuit he's wearing is unzipped all the way, with the sleeves tied around his waist, leaving his muscled chest open for inspection. Shame he's still wearing a t-shirt, although it's wet enough with sweat that he could win competitions in pubs.

He's lugging a backpack that is close buckling under the strain of its contents. Once clear of the plinth, he shrugs out of it and lets it down to the ground with a loud muffled clunking. "There are even some more tiles hidden under the gravel."

"Bloody 'ell, your old man was busy."

"It took him years from what he was able to tell me."

"Yeah, now that's what I don't understand. If he could tell you how he did it, why couldn't he tell you where the bleeding 'ell he'd stowed them?"

"The timing of his death was rather, ah unfortunate. I only had minutes with him before he passed."

Liam acts uncomfortable to be discussing this and after what Eadie had told Stef about how Arthur shuffled off, she can't altogether blame him.

"Where's your mum in all of this?"

"Couldn't stand the shame of how father died. Took her own life not long after."

Sheesh, as embarrassing as her dad can be after a few pints, he's never done anything that would have her mum topping herself.

"That can't have been easy."

"It wasn't. So you can understand why I'm not keen on my uncle risking the same method of demise."

"Not dying on my watch, that's for bleedin' sure. I've even got a handle on mouth-to-mouth."

Liam pausing on his unpacking of the backpack and arches a brow. "Have you now?"

"Not like that, ya dirty sod." Stef's unable to stop the giggle that follows.

"Right!" says Liam, suddenly straightening from his task. "Let's call it a day."

Stef doesn't need any encouragement to abandon the floor, even if she's surprised they're stopping early for the day. Well, earlier than the previous two days, but not soon enough in her books. Barmaid work is easy compared to this.

Stef's not long been in the tub with the water deep enough she could learn scuba in here, when the door to her bathroom swings open. Liam walks in as though it's this most usual thing in the world. It's not as far as she's concerned and she makes quick work of corralling the bubbles until they're covering all the bits they should be.

This proves futile when Liam shrugs out of the robe he's wearing, showing himself to be starkers, and steps into the other end of the tub.

"Don't look at me like that. I wasn't the one who used all the hot water."

Stef's got two choices.

She can get out of the tub and leave the room in a huff.

Or she can threaten to do him damage if he comes down her end of the tub.

Tired as she is, she opts for the latter. Let's be honest, the bloke is easy on the eye and he's loaded to boot.

Maybe it's time to retire her whip.

Or not.

Liam's a little too cheeky for her liking. He needs someone to take him in hand. Or take a hand to him. Either works for Stef and the smile she's getting in return suggests he won't be averse.

Hmmm, it must be hereditary.

THANK YOU

For choosing my book from all those fantastic Chick Lit stories out there! It's readers like you who allow me to pursue my career as a writer.

Lastly, don't be a stranger, if you check out my website you can sign up for my bi-monthly newsletter.

This is chock full of new releases, special offers and some fabulous competitions.

There might even be one or two cat photos.

www.andrenelowauthor.com

ABOUT THE AUTHOR

Andrene, or Andie as her cozy mystery readers know her, has a love of writing instilled in her by her mother. Although, if her mum was still alive, she'd be smacking Andrene across the back of the head given the direction some of her writing has taken.

Irreverent, cutting and reflecting her background as a stand-up comic, it's edgy and chock full of humour that can be very dark in places. She also enjoys a good bit of snark.

Andie lives in New Zealand in the beautiful Hawke's Bay - an area renowned for its stunning scenery and award-winning wines.

Also available as Wingspan Pocket Editions

Andrene's cozy mystery series writing as 'Andie Low'.

She's a jinxed witch with Bruce Lee moves, he's her snarky Jack Russell. Together they're out to rid the magical world of those who would do bad, oh and not die while they're at it.

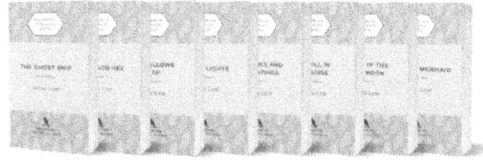

If you're interested, here are three chapters of The Ghost Ship, the first in this series. Please note this series is written using American English.

Frankie B
The Ghost Ship

Andie Low

Squabbling Sparrows Press

She's a jinxed witch with Bruce Lee moves. He's her snarky, telepathic Jack Russell. They're out to rid their coven of the ghost ship, without dying.

Not yet over the loss of her mom, jinxed witch Frankie B is in a new city, without family, a home or her full powers. Thank goodness for Dex, her muffin-loving, snarky Jack Russell familiar.

After being evicted, they're faced with moving into a flea-pit motel, when Dex spots a vacancy at a nearby marina. But this is no ordinary marina, and before they've even had time to finish unpacking, life takes a deadly turn.

Will Frankie solve the mystery of the missing witches and rid the coven of the ghost of Captain Russell Garnet? Or will her ability to make him corporeal see her stuck as his prisoner until her dying breath?

Either way, she isn't going down without a fight and with her Bruce Lee moves and Dex and Zane, her mysterious — but drop-dead gorgeous — neighbor, helping how can she fail?

All names, characters, places, and incidents in this publication are fictitious or are used fictitiously. Any resemblance to real persons, living or dead, events or locales is entirely coincidental.

© Andrene Low 2018

All rights reserved. No part of this text may be reproduced or transmitted in any form or by any means, including photocopying, recording, or other electronic or mechanical methods, without the express written permission of the author or publisher, except in the case of brief quotations embodied in critical reviews and certain other non-commercial uses permitted by copyright law.

For information regarding permission, email the author at andrenelow@andrenelowauthor.com, subject line: Permission

1

Looking up briefly from her late mom's big book of spells, Frankie checks progress on the dusting and vacuuming. The spell — page 795 — has taken ages to perfect and works like something out of the Sorcerer's Apprentice, hold those buckets of water.

Despite being twenty-five, Frankie isn't good at housework — or magic — and so the hours spent perfecting the housework spells have been worth it. If Mrs Bryson her — eighty if she's a day — landlady, is as picky with tomorrow's 'surprise' spot-check as she has been every other week, Frankie wants to give her no cause for complaint.

She knows she's being paranoid, but with cheap accommodation scarce in Seattle, eviction would be a disaster. Sleeping in her car sucks.

It hadn't taken long to twig Mrs Bryson only ever drops in unannounced on Sunday morning on her way home from church. Frankie now cleans on Saturday afternoon, giving herself as little time as possible to mess the place up.

The first check came close to ending in disaster. Dexter, her Jack Russell — who isn't on the lease because of a strict *no-pets* policy — was asleep on the rug in the lounge, legs in the air and snoring to rouse the dead.

Panicked, Frankie performed a spell for putting her washing away; zapping him from the lounge to the beat up Toyota she inherited from her mom. She'd been lucky given it was half a block away. After this nasty surprise, she put a *doorbell* ward on the apartment complex's courtyard alerting her to the landlady's presence.

Frankie settles herself deeper into the junkyard sofa — part of the rental's *high-end* furnishings — doing her best to avoid the dodgy springs. She taps her E-reader, turning the page, ready to get on with her studies. Thank the Goddess her mom had performed the conversion spell, because if it had been down to Frankie, the device would have been fried.

Converting the original book had been a no-brainer. Because of its large size and weight Frankie can only read it at the table, and she prefers the sofa. The device also allows her to concentrate on memorizing the spells without thoughts of her mom swamping her. Simply turning pages on the large book has hints of her mom's favorite perfume enveloping her, with Frankie in tears soon after.

Unforgiving sofa aside, this corner of the lounge is the perfect spot to read, with sunlight flooding in and a gentle breeze blowing through the wide-open French doors.

She isn't sure how much time has passed when there's octogenarian screeching from behind the sofa. "What on earth is that disgusting flea-bag doing lying on my good rug?"

Frankie doesn't bother turning the E-reader off, tossing it on the coffee table, twisting her legs around and clambering to her feet. Never mind the old crone's dodged the ward in the courtyard, she's a full day early.

"Mrs Bryson, I can explain." Frankie isn't

sure how, but is going give it her best shot. The place has been too hard-won to risk getting kicked out. Not when she's still trying to find a job that will give her enough spare time to practice her craft as she promised her mom. Frankie still doesn't believe her life is in danger, but a promise is a promise.

"I might be old, but I'm not blind." The old girl having missed the ancient vacuum cleaner and feather duster working away without human intervention rather disproves this. Perhaps it's that her attention is on Dex, who's sitting as at attention as Frankie is standing.

"We're doomed." Dexter's voice is loud inside Frankie's head, with their ability to communicate telepathically a gift from Frankie's mom. With the other tenants in Frankie's apartment block complaining bitterly about his constant barking, it was this or move. Turns out he hadn't liked the synthetic nature of his dog bed, saying it lit up like the fourth of July if he moved too fast. The fluffy, nylon bedding being replaced with Egyptian cotton made him a happy pup.

Now all Frankie has to deal with is the small dog's incessant chatter and propensity to hum.

"I'm looking after the dog for ah, a friend. He's going home this afternoon. I'll ah, vacuum the place until it's spotless." As tempting as it is to tell the old battle-ax the apartment will be even cleaner than when they'd moved in, Frankie buttons her lips.

She's said too much. This brief mention of the vacuum has her landlady noticing the household appliance working away on its own. It's even getting into the corners and under the battered and dinged sideboard.

"It's, it's, it's." Mrs Bryson collapses in a pile of purple velour tracksuit, white hair, and rickety bones. Not that she's down there for long with Frankie manhandling her up onto the sofa where she'll be safe from the vacuum cleaner. The be-spelled device, having picked up on Frankie's agitated state, has doubled its efforts to find every speck of dust in the place.

Frankie's packed their belongings in the Toyota and is sneaking out the French doors after Dex when Mrs Bryson regains full consciousness.

So much for avoiding a big scene.

Frankie knows there's no staying following this afternoon's debacle. Never mind Dex, *Nor-*

mals don't appreciate witchcraft even when it's being used for as mundane a task as housework.

Mrs Bryson escorts Dex and Frankie to the car, berating them every step of the way, whilst making the sign of the cross and giving them the evil eye. If Mrs Bryson was packing holy water, they'd be wet by now.

Safely away from the curb, with no clue as to their destination, Frankie takes a quick peek in the rearview mirror. Mrs Bryson is shaking her fist so violently in their direction, she nearly falls over. If she did, she'd no doubt blame this on Frankie, too.

"Old bag. She should have paid us to stay there. I doubt it's ever been as clean and tidy."

"Not true," says Dex, who's riding *shotgun*. *"While you were packing, I peed on the mat in the kitchen."*

Frankie can't hold back a splutter of laughter. "Why did you do that?"

Busy scratching behind his ear, he takes his time answering. *"She said I had fleas."*

Frankie looks at him, an eyebrow raised.

"I caught them from her rug!"

And while this might be true, it doesn't

change their current predicament. They're back to where they were when they'd first arrived in Seattle. Homeless, and with even less cash to splash.

"I guess we'll find a cheap motel for tonight and search for a new apartment tomorrow. Not that we'll find one as cheap."

"Or nasty," pipes up Dex.

Dex pulls his head back inside the car, licking his lips free of wind-induced drool. He drops onto the seat and turns to Frankie. *"Any chance of a pit-stop?"*

"Sorry dude. I was thinking."

She's thinking back on how different her life had been six months earlier. Before her mom, who was driving Frankie's car, got shunted in front of a speeding freight train. The police never found the culprit although the evidence pointed to them driving a red pickup. Shame her mom's ability to see the future hadn't allowed her to avoid the accident altogether.

From a life full of love and laughter,

Frankie's world became so dark she couldn't see a way forward. Gone were the days of helping her mom, Pat, with the day-to-day running of the Patsy's Magic Emporium. Gone was the laughter. Gone was the security.

It was at the hospital that Frankie's life nose-dived. During a moment of lucidity, her mother warned her to get far, far away. Her final words were to tell Frankie her life was in danger. With her mom then slipping into a coma from which she'd never awaken, Frankie didn't get to hear why.

Attributing the raving to the head injury her mom had sustained, Frankie did her best to get on with her life. Her move into the small apartment over the magic emporium was her first mistake, with the space bombarding her with constant reminders of her mom. Then the shop had faltered, due to her being nowhere near as talented a witch and medium. As if all this wasn't enough, Jason, her boyfriend of two years then dumped her because her constant tears were "bumming him out".

Heart-sore and weary, Frankie decided leaving town was a good idea.

"In here! In here! Pull in here!" Dexter's excited telepathic shouting is enough to have Frankie's concentration back on the road. She swerves into a parking lot next to a marina a second later.

Before she's had time to engage the handbrake, Dex flies out the window and over to the nearest pole as fast as he can with his back legs crossed. His sigh of relief inside her head is loud and heart-felt.

While she waits for him to finish his business and sniff every other upright surface in a one hundred foot radius, Frankie checks out their surroundings. Across the road there's collection of shops and trades. There's even a café. One of the narrowest Frankie has ever seen, with it being not much wider than the front door itself. It's a true hole-in-the-wall establishment.

Frankie climbs out of the car, leaning back in to grab her handbag. "Dex, can you guard the car while I go get a coffee?"

"Yeah, sure, whatever." He doesn't bother lifting his head from a patch of grass he's sniffing as though his life depends on it.

"And something to eat!" says Frankie.

His head comes up as though spring-mounted. *"Blueberry muffin for me,"* he gets out before returning to his sniffing.

Frankie threads her way through a motley collection of parked cars and, after checking for traffic, crosses the road to the café. Its name has her smiling.

Magic Beans - Proprietor: Mac Fletcher? Well, it appears Mac has a sense of humor.

Back at the marina, she takes a seat on a bench facing the water and rips open the paper bag that holds her and Dexter's muffins. He always has blueberry while her favorite is anything with chocolate. Her first sip of coffee leaves her transfixed.

Magic Beans is right. Even with Seattle's reputation for good coffee, it's the best *Cup of Jo* she's had since arriving in the city. It's rich, velvety and without a hint of bitterness. That the barista has sprinkled chocolate on top is the icing on the ah, coffee.

She's demolished her muffin and is half way through her coffee before Dex returns. He's covered in cobwebs and grinning like a loon.

"What's got you looking so happy?"

"I know something you don't know," he sings, settling himself on the bench and getting stuck into his muffin as though he hasn't eaten in days.

"Well, don't leave me hanging, buddy."

A muffled *"hang on a sec"* makes its way inside her head, forcing Frankie to wait for her loyal sidekick to finish his snack. He's still licking his chops when he jumps off the seat and trots away. He's covered a good distance before he looks back. *"Well, aren't you coming?"*

"Hang on."

Frankie swallows the last of the coffee, and on her way to join her familiar, chucks the cup and bag in a trash can. She's only just caught up with him, when he plonks himself on the boardwalk and looks up.

It takes a second for Frankie to register what's caught the small dog's attention. There's a sign nailed to a pole about a houseboat for rent on *Pier 51*. It's only $100 a week, pets are welcome, and it's currently vacant.

"Sounds too good to be true! Wait?" She looks from the sign to Dex. "You can read?"

Dex shrugs as though it's no big deal. *"Hey, I have to do something when you're out."*

"Righty-ho. Let's go get us a home." Frankie rips the sign off the pole, and having found the right pier is soon striding down the dock with Dex trotting beside her, humming.

2

Her footsteps echoing on the wooden boards, Frankie's thoughts are in a tangle. What if the place is a hovel? It leaks? It's half submerged? She's not expecting much for $100 a week, although maybe not as bad as what's parked in slip number thirty-two. The rusty shipping container that's plopped askew on an even rustier barge is a maritime disaster on speed dial.

Did she read the number wrong?

Dex, who's on the side deck of this homage to corrosion, interrupts her thoughts. *"Nope, it's the right place."*

With nothing to lose, Frankie wanders along the floating dock that sits between *The Crate* — as she thinks of the place — and the *Jolly Roger*, a large cruiser. Frankie knocks on the frosted glass door cut into the side of the container, waiting without luck for someone to answer. She's given up, when she spots a small note stuck in the doorframe. The spidery writing and lack of spaces make it a slow read.

> *Welcomeaboard.*
> *Pleasegotothe*
> *houseboatopposite*
> *forthekey.Gxx*

All that's missing are the hash tags.

After making sense of the scrawl, Frankie's shoulders drop in defeat. "Hecking heck, it looks like it's gone."

Dex looks up from his forensic examination of the deck, *"It's been let?"*

"Looks to be."

"I hate motels. They have fleas."

Watching Dex plodding the length of the barge, stopping now and then to sniff something, Frankie thinks on motels they can afford. Somewhere they'll avoid being eaten alive, but that will be better than a night in the Toyota. *Perhaps if she flea-bombs the place before they move their stuff in?*

She's Googling accommodation options on

her phone when a hatch opens on the front of the cruiser and an older man pops his head out. "Are you here about renting the *Shangri La*?"

The Shangri La? Is he kidding?

Only by sucking hard on her lips is Frankie able to hold in her guffaw. "Yes, although I see it's been let."

"No. Not that I'm aware? Name's Jack, by-the-by."

That he doesn't have Captain tacked onto the front is a let-down, what with him wearing a captain's hat and all. Frankie suspects that if she could see the rest, there'd be navy whites and lots of medals involved.

"Hi. I'm Frankie. Frankie B."

"And may I ask what the B stands for?"

Frankie isn't sure why she doesn't make something up, but she's incapable of lying about this one thing. Not that she lies about much else. Well, apart from being vague about Dex, her *room-mate,* when she's applying for new apartments.

"It's B for Bonny."

Wait for it. Wait for it.

She's heard the lot. Bonny and Clyde. Bonny Doon — the place and the band. Even 'bonny wee thing', in an appalling Scottish accent.

"As in Anne Bonny, the pirate?" Jack's face is alight with excitement.

"Ah, yes, but how did…"

Before she can get the rest of her question out, Jack says, "Welcome aboard," gives her a jaunty salute and disappears back through the hatch.

"That was weird," says Frankie, to Dex who's trying to inch his way around the lattice at the end of the rusty metal box. "If you fall in, I am NOT fishing you out."

No one ever mentions Anne Bonny. Everything but.

Her frown transforms into a wide grin. The place is still available. At least until something better comes along. It'll be a step-up from a flea-pit motel, and a heap better than the Toyota. At least she hopes so, because she hasn't been able to check out the interior, with the door being frosted and the windows skinny and near the roof line.

Back on the main pier, Frankie approaches the gorgeous houseboat that's tied up opposite. The cherry-red front door, with its creepy brass octopus knocker, is intimidating, no doubt on purpose. Not that this stops Frankie from grabbing a handful of tentacles and knocking hard enough she may as well be tenderizing them ready for the grill.

While waiting, she takes in the other boats and houseboats, with her gaze coming to rest on a stunning double-masted schooner. Its length is such that it takes up the whole dock that forms a tee at the end of the main pier. The *American Pearl* must be worth millions.

She's looking at it when the door next to her opens.

After this Frankie's robbed of her ability to speak, with the thief in question standing at least six-three, with a body many in Hollywood would kill for. Even though he's dressed in a baggy white t-shirt and faded jeans, he has her mouth drier than Death Valley at the height of summer. Maybe she's seen him in a movie or an advertisement? She can't work out what it is, but she gets the sense she's already met him.

His handsome face marred by a frown that knots his brows, he crosses his arms over what looks to be a solid chest while leaning against the door frame. The pose shrieks 'SCRAM'.

Incapable of speech, or even rational

thought, Frankie holds the tattered 'TO LET' sign up so he can see it.

The change in him is instantaneous. He pushes himself away from the wall with his shoulder, straightens and turning around, grabs a key off a side table in the hall. He holds it up by its yellow ribbon, lifting it higher when Frankie tries to take it from him.

"What's your name, *Shortcake*?"

Shortcake? Is he serious?

Frankie checks her outfit to see if it's morphed into something pink and frilly. Nope, she's still wearing no-nonsense boots, jeans with holes in the knees and a dark gray tee-shirt. She runs her fingers through her hair, messing the short, spikey style. She tugs a lock forward and checks if it's still the fiery red she loves so much. *Yep*.

She returns his gaze with a scowl. "Name's Frankie."

"And who is this?"

The key stuffed in his pocket, he crouches and tickles Dex under the chin. It's something that'd normally have the small dog trying to relieve the tickler of a finger, or two. Instead, Dex drops and rolls onto his back like a lady of the night looking for extra income.

"*Oh, don't stop, don't stop, don't stop,*" Dex mumbles telepathically. Watching the guy rubbing his large hand up and down the dog's tummy is doing funny things to Frankie's own.

"Sorry buddy, that's all I've got time for. I've got things to do and your mom needs to look at the *Shangri La*."

After giving Dex's tummy a final flourish, he gets back to his feet and digs around in his pocket for the key. Once again, he dangles it by the ribbon, but this time instead of trying to take it off him; Frankie holds her hand out and waits for him to drop it in her palm. She's not playing his stupid games, no matter how good-looking he is.

"Thanks. I'll take a look."

Frankie stalks down his gang plank, over the pier and onto *The Crate*. She's conscious of him watching her every step, and it takes every ounce of her will-power not to give into the temptation to sneak a peek back. Not that Dex has any issues casting longing looks.

Frankie slides the frosted glass door open, preparing herself for the worst. With the outside not in the running for any Architectural Digest

Awards she's expecting hideous carpet, tatty furniture, and a bathroom behind a curtain.

At least she hopes there's a curtain.

And a bathroom.

"Wow!"

The floors are bamboo and there's a double cabin bed dressed like something out of a home catalog. To her left there's a table and chairs and a sectional sofa, with a kitchenette and flat-pack armoire against the wall opposite. Everything looks to be brand new.

There's a bathroom, tucked to the side of the cabin bed and — oh happy days — it's got a door. While tiny, the bathroom still has a walk-in shower, commode, and vanity.

There isn't a soaking tub.

There will be once Frankie moves in.

Back in the main cabin Frankie spots Dex spread out on a fluffy sheepskin rug in front of double glass doors that lead to a small back deck. Yep, he likes the place too.

"Dex! Wake up, slug. You can't move in until I've signed a lease."

The only response she gets is snuffling as the small dog settles himself even deeper into the sheepskin rug. He's out of luck if he thinks she'll leave him where he is.

"If you come back with me, you might get another tummy rub."

Heck, even she wouldn't mind one of those.

It's just the catalyst he needs, and Dex is on his feet and halfway across the pier before Frankie's had time to lock the door.

The ugly octopus having received another hammering, Frankie doesn't have to wait this time, with the door swinging wide, as though *The Hunk* has been lurking in the hallway.

She doesn't give him time to call her *Shortcake* again. "I'll..." She clears her throat and starts again. "I'll take it."

"Excellent. I've got a copy of the lease inside."

To be alone with this guy is something she'd prefer to avoid. She's not sure what it is about him that has her on edge, but she's not going to ignore it like she did with her ex. Even knowing at least two defensive spells, she can't use them without outing herself as a witch and bang would go the rental.

Not that she's altogether helpless without her magic. With her dad gone by the time she was two, she'd spent her childhood living in neighborhoods her mom could afford; with these often being so far on the wrong side of the tracks you couldn't hear the trains even if you tried. This was why she'd joined an after-school program, allowing her to do her homework in peace and not to a soundtrack of street fights and domestic violence.

It was there she'd met her own Mr Miyagi, and while she hadn't learned karate, she'd learned something she thinks is better. Jeet Kune Do is the perfect martial art for women and Frankie figures if it was good enough for Bruce Lee, then it's good enough for her. The one maneuver she isn't keen on is the one where you jab someone in the eyes. On purpose! Even thinking on it gives her the heebie jeebies.

Maybe today would be the day? Mind you, this would mean they'd miss out on the lease, too.

He moves to the side, and motions for her to enter, something she does after a moment's hesitation. It's not that she can sense danger emanating from him, but more that she's not keen on getting up close and personal with this much testosterone.

Turning until she has her back to the wall, she waits for him to close the front door.

The Hunk clicks his fingers and for a second Frankie thinks she's being given the hurry-up.

"Come on, buddy, in you come."

"Dex, his name is Dex." Frankie looks at her small pal, who's slipped between them and is trotting down the middle of the hall. He looks back every couple of steps to confirm he's okay being indoors.

The front door closed, *The Hunk* walks past Frankie, overtakes Dex and swings a door open at the end of the hallway, flooding the dark space with sunlight. After inching her way into the room Frankie has to wait for her eyes to adjust to the extra light. She's then held spellbound. While the view from *The Crate* is of boats and an industrial park, the view here is magical. There's a wide expanse of water and the Seattle skyline in the distance, meaning it would be spectacular at night.

A polite cough has Frankie turning to see him standing next to a sleek glass table, with the lease there, a ballpoint pen on top.

"Oh right."

He pulls out a chair for her, and only when she's sitting, does he pull one out for himself.

Broken broomsticks, Frankie would prefer he made himself busy somewhere else than sit and stare at her while she ploughs her way through a whole stack of legalese.

After reading the first couple of clauses and conscious of his inspection, she scans rather than reads the rest of the first page. Things only slow down when she turns the single sheet of paper over. Looking at the spot at the bottom where she's supposed to sign, two things become obvious. First off, her full name already being listed on the document shrieks of magic. Secondly, she doubts the guy sitting opposite her is Gwen Rasmussen.

3

What's going on? Frankie looks from the lease, to the guy sitting opposite and back. The familiar sensation of magic tingling in her fingers has her dropping her hands to her lap where she's less likely to set fire to something. Or worse.

"Who are you? Because I doubt your name is Gwen." Rubbing her hands on her jeans, Frankie disperses the spell that's arisen due to her agitation.

"I'm Zane, a friend of Gwen's. She's out of town, so she left the key with me."

"And how is it that my full name is showing on the lease?"

"You'd have to ask Gwen that."

Frankie isn't sure what to do. With the

missing Gwen having signed the lease, all she has to do to make *The Crate* hers is to sign, too. Only problem is that with her full name there in black and white, it smacks of magic. Magic failure she might be, but even she knows you don't sign a magical contract without knowing who and what.

Hexed hopping rabbits.

"I can't sign this. Not without meeting Gwen."

Frankie places the key on top of the lease, pushes her chair back and gets to her feet.

"Come on Dex, time to go."

He isn't as quick to do her bidding as she'd like, prompting her to clap her hands and tell him to move it.

"But I don't want to stay in a motel." He drags his feet along the hallway.

"Hang on a second." Zane strides by Dex and her, putting his hand on the door to stop her opening it. "What say you move into the *Shangri La* and sign the lease when Gwen is back? That work?"

"Hot dang!" Dex bounces and spins on the spot in his excitement at not having to spend the night in a flea-bag motel. *"Say yes! Say yes!"*

. . .

Frankie can't see a downside to Zane's suggestion, apart from living opposite him that is. There's something about him that draws her in. Like an old boyfriend you still think is cute, but who you know is bad news.

Back at the car, it dawns on her she hadn't even locked it when she'd gone off with Dex earlier. A frantic search shows everything is still where it should be, including her MP3 player plugged into the car stereo. She's heard stories about the types who hang around in parking lots waiting for someone to be stupid enough to leave their car unlocked. "Phew, that was lucky."

After placing the parking sticker Zane has given her on the dash, Frankie readies herself to grab as many bags as she can in one go. Anything to avoid a zillion trips from the car to *The Crate*. And no, she is not calling that rusty heap of metal the *Shangri La*. It's the most ludicrous and inappropriate name, ever.

"*Oy, this work?*" Dex is on the far side of the parking lot standing next to what looks to be an old-fashioned mail cart. He's right; it'll be perfect for ferrying the weird assortment that makes up their worldly goods.

"It might belong to someone."

"So, we're only borrowing it."

"That's the lot." Frankie plonks a large, dark-brown leather suitcase atop everything else crammed in the wheeled cart. The case belonged to her late dad and — along with her fiery locks and the amulet that hangs around her neck — is all she has of his.

"Can I get on? Can I? Can I?" Dex bounces on the spot showing his enthusiasm at taking a ride in anything with wheels, even if it's only an old mail cart.

"Sure you can." Bending, Frankie scoops him up and places him atop her dad's case, where he sits in splendor as she wheels everything to their new home.

They're not even halfway along the pier before Dex is standing on the suitcase, leaning forward and urging Frankie to greater speed by barking out, *"Faster! Faster!"*, inside her head.

"If I go any faster, you're getting wet." Yet again, Frankie yanks on the cart to straighten it.

Courtesy of the zigzag path, it takes longer than it should to see their belongings in *The Crate*. Now all Frankie wants is a cup of tea and a power-nap. Shame their kettle is still sitting on the counter at the old apartment. Without a key — and with Mrs Bryson most likely still trying to stop the vacuum and net the feather duster while waiting for an exorcist — nipping back to retrieve it isn't an option.

"Guess I need to go buy a new one."

"*You forgot my bowl, too,*" says Dex, from the sheepskin rug he's claimed as his own.

"Hex it!" Grabbing her phone out of her handbag she does a quick search to see where the nearest supermarket is. She's so shattered it could be next door and still not close enough. "It's not too far away. Will you be okay on your own?"

"*Sure.*" Dex lies on his side on the sheepskin rug and stretches his legs as much as possible before folding them tight against his body. Following a small tweak to the angle of his head, he shuts his eyes, dismissing her.

Back at *The Crate* a short time later, Frankie drops her shopping just inside the door, shocked to find Dex chatting away to three new friends.

"*Frankie, meet Jojo, Stinky, and Spud.*" Dex nods at a Siamese cat, a hamster, and a small pig in turn. And the pig's small as in not crowding eight inches at the shoulder, meaning Spud is either a runt or he's had help of the magical variety.

"Greetings."

"Hello."

"Pleased to meet you."

Okay, with her able to hear them all, it looks as if it isn't only the pig that's been bespelled. Not that she can fault the manners of the trio.

Frankie's thinking on how to get rid of her unwanted guests when Jojo, the Siamese, tilts her head to the side *"Mom wants me. Bye."* She disappears in a shower of sparks.

Stinky and Spud don't even say goodbye before disappearing, too.

"Where did they come from?"

"They're locals, from the pier."

"Okay, so now I know where they live. How come they were here?"

"Oh, I was thinking it would be nice to have a few friends. And poof, they're here."

This confirms for Frankie she's not the only person with special skills on *Pier 51* and Dex isn't the only familiar. It's either this or Dex has magical abilities she's been unaware of. Frankie isn't sure about being part of a group like this. Her mom avoided it at all costs.

The kettle on to boil, Frankie sets to emptying her dad's suitcase. This takes longer than it should on the face of it because of the case being magical and able to hold as much as one five times the size. By the time it's empty, her bed is all but buried by a weird assortment of clothing.

While some items are hers, the majority is stuff she's kept to remind her of people who are no longer in her life. Frankie finds far more comfort in burying her face in a much-worn article of clothing than in looking at a flat photo.

Jason is the only person whose clothes she hasn't held onto, with her having burned anything he'd left at her place. His neighbors had been furious about the bonfire in the middle of his front lawn, but Frankie found it rather cathartic.

She even took marshmallows.

Even without opening the closet, she knows she hasn't got a hope of fitting everything in there. She stands before it, going through the spell in her head in a practice run before holding her hands up ready to get to work.

"Oy! Stop."

"Wait? What? Why?" Frankie looks at Dex and drops her hands to her sides.

"Remember last time you did magic with the doors open?"

"Good point. Thanks buddy."

Only after locking the frosted glass door and drawing the drapes to the deck tight, does Frankie lift her hands again.

Wardrobe, cupboard,
closet, chest
I need more space
to hold my best
With lots of rails
and heaps of room
to hang my hat
and store my broom.

Frankie doesn't even own a hat or broom, but figures if a spell ain't broke, don't fix it. When the magic has built up enough, she points at the closet and sparks stream from her fingers, leaving the armoire looking bedazzled. Only after the last spark has fallen to the floor does she open the doors and step inside.

The space is perfect, with lots of hanging space and two sets of drawers, ideal for smaller items. There's even a large, freestanding unit in the middle of the room with shoe storage underneath and a velvet upholstered top perfect for holding jewelry and other trinkets. Shame Frankie doesn't own any bling. Not that she'd wear it if she did. It's not her style.

The only other enclosed space is the bathroom and a quick sizing spell transforms this, too. No longer a glorified broom cupboard, it now smacks more of high-end spa, and the soaking tub is a beauty. Frankie's wise enough to know she hasn't magicked the tub out of thin air and that it's had to come from somewhere.

Not keen on taking something someone might need, she visualizes a summer or winter house where the bath won't be missed for the night. She also makes sure she returns it's sparkling and in perfect order. From time-to-time she even sends one back in better order than it's arrived. Sure, it'll lead to head scratching when the owners see the bath is cleaner and that the chip by the plug hole has repaired itself. This she can live with.

Her cup of tea abandoned in favor of putting everything away, Frankie's still folding and hanging when there's a booming knock on the side of the container. As tempting as it would be to magic the rest away, she's still hit-and-miss — mostly misses — when it comes to free-spelling. With her luck her favorites will end up in the closet at their ratty old apartment.

Rather than look like she's up to something shady, Frankie closes the closet and opens the drapes. She unlocks the frosted glass door and slides it open; unsure who the visitor will be, with no one knowing she's living here.

Apart from Zane that is.

He holds his arms wide, a bottle of bubbles in his left hand and two champagne flutes in his right. "Welcome to the marina." His smile is as wide as his gesture.

"Don't you think this is a tad premature?" Frankie places herself in the doorway, blocking him from entering. "I haven't signed the lease yet."

"But you will." His tone is self-assured.

His manner has Frankie bristling. What was it her mom used to say about guys like him? That's right, "Why buy a book when you can join the library."

They're at an impasse until Frankie notices small blue sparks filling the space between them.

Gah, he's a witch, warlock, or even worse, a sleaze like Jason. *Why hadn't she sensed that when she was with him earlier?* And hex it if he doesn't look to be trying to spell her into letting him come inside.

Her hands up in a defensive position, Frankie doesn't hold back. Not that she hits him with magic because she doesn't know a 'heave a hunk in the harbor' hex. Instead, she throws her weight forward, hitting him solidly in the solar plexus, and shoving hard.

The only bit of magic she uses is a simple levitation spell she learned as a child that sees her holding the bottle and glasses when he surfaces.

"Next time you try that rubbish, I won't hold back."

She's inching her way through the side door with her spoils of war when he launches himself out of the water. That he lands on the pier after completing a double somersault tells her that whatever he is, he's strong. His wet clothes molding to his body like they are tells her he's got an eight-pack that would give Ryan Reynolds some competition.

With that type of power at his fingertips, maybe she shouldn't have been as rough. She's worrying about being hurt if he retaliates when she sees him break into a broad grin after which he licks his lips slowly and deliberately. It looks like harming her is the last thing on his mind. Wonky wands, with part of her still hurting from Jason's rejection, this is even scarier.

After sliding the door shut with her hip, she wastes no time plonking the bubbles and glasses on the table. With her hands free, she spins around and locks the door. After a second's pause, she throws up a ward designed to keep him away. It's big enough to enclose *The Crate* entirely.

Ward spell training was the one thing her mom had refused to back down on. She'd made Frankie practice until she could create one without thinking. And without need to say an incantation. Nope, just thinking about the words works for these.

The question is despite all that training,

will her ward be strong enough to keep him at bay?

The bigger question is does she want it to?

I hope you enjoyed this short peek at this series. Add them to your Wingspan Pocket Edition collection soon. Because who doesn't love the books on their shelves matching?

Lightning Source UK Ltd.
Milton Keynes UK
UKHW020501160920
369943UK00010B/347